Jumbles Wood

WHEN THE ANIMALS
WENT TO WAR

For Amy and Hannah, who helped inspire this story and Patricia who
gave me the time to write it

BY DAVID SKENTELBERY

Illustrations by Patricia Skentelbery

First published 2007

Orbit Publishing

The New Media Centre

Old Road

Warrington, Cheshire WA4 1AT

ISBN 978-0-9556778-0-9

INTRODUCTION

In this book you will meet the animals of Jumbles Wood, including Blink Otter

Now, when it comes to rivers and streams, lakes and anything to do with water, Blink is an expert.

But in some other ways, he is not very clever – which is why even his friends sometimes call him a "Silly Otter."

One of the things Blink is not very good at is understanding the meaning of words. He is always asking the other animals what they mean when they use a word he hasn't heard before.

If you come across any words you haven't heard of before, and can't work out what they mean, do what Blink does. Ask someone.

Fortunately, one of the other characters in this book is very good with words. But even he carries a dictionary with him, in case he comes across a word he doesn't know.

His name is Old Crow, and while he can be a bit crotchety at times, he is quite a nice fellow really and will usually help out.

At the back of this book you will find some of the words in Old Crow's dictionary which Blink has problems with, together with what they mean. Old Crow won't mind if you check them out.

You can find out what is going on in Jumbles Wood any time you like by visiting the website

www.jumbleswood.com

There you will find pictures of the wood and the main characters in the story. You can even send them an email – and get a reply!

CHAPTER 1

A stranger calls

Snuff Rabbit reached the end of a chapter, carefully placed a leaf between the pages to mark the place and closed his book. He yawned, looked up at his Grandfather clock, which was ticking away ponderously in a corner of his little parlour, and sighed.

"Time to go to bed," he said to himself. And no-one answered, because there was no-one else there in Snuff's little house.

"I'll just put the milk bottles out and lock-up," said Snuff Rabbit, who never minded whether there was anyone to listen to him or not.

He bobbed into the kitchen, picked up the two shiny, empty bottles that he had thoroughly washed after his supper, and scurried along the passage to his front door.

Snuff Rabbit's house was, like that of most rabbits, underground. The door was almost hidden by long grass and the roots of a huge oak tree, known throughout Jumbles Wood as Snuff's Oak.

All the animals in Jumbles Wood knew Snuff, so there was a well-beaten path to his front door. His back door was less well known, for it was even more secretly hidden in grass nearly 20 yards away from the oak.

"I hope Blink Otter won't be late with the milk in the morning," said Snuff, still talking to himself as he put the two milk bottles down on his step. "I've a lot to do tomorrow so I want an early breakfast."

He paused on the step and took a deep breath on the warm, evening air. He sniffed appreciatively as the scent of wild flowers reached his little pink nostrils and his whiskers twitched.

Jumbles Wood

"It's beautiful," he sighed.

"Oh, b-b-bother!" said a voice.

"Bother what?" inquired Snuff, unaware for a moment that someone was butting in on his conversation with himself. "There's nothing to bother anyone on a lovely night like this."

"D-d-drat it!" insisted the voice. And then there was a scurrying and scratching noise, followed by a distinct and very definite BOMP!

The bomping sound was followed by a muffled "OOOOF!" and then a less violent BUMP which Snuff Rabbit, from his own experience, identified as a furry sit-upon being sat upon suddenly and rather hard.

"Oooooh!" said the voice.

Snuff peered into the gloom.

"Who's there?" he called, nervously.

"Who's w-w-where?" came a rather shaky reply from the darkness.

"W-w-what's more, where's where? And where am I?"

Snuff could make little sense of the muffled mutterings that came out of the darkness. He could see nothing. He could only hear nonsensical murmuring and heavy breathing and the scrabbling of small feet.

He opened his door wider to let the light from the oil lamp in his hall stream out. But still he could see nothing.

"Who's there? Can you see me?" he called again.

"Ah!" said the voice. "A light in the d-d-darkness."

Snuff stared out into the darkness, straining his eyes for any sign of the owner of the strange voice. But still he could see nothing. Then he heard small feet pattering swiftly, saw a blurred movement in the gloom and, before he could say so much as Jack Robinson....BOMP!

Something small, rounded and furry, struck Snuff Rabbit in the middle of his equally rounded and furry stomach. A small, whiskered face with big brown eyes appeared before his startled gaze and without more ado he was bowled over backwards to land on his own sit-upon on his own doormat.

"Oh! Good Grief!" he exclaimed.

"Botheration!" said the other voice.

Slowly, Snuff Rabbit collected his scattered wits together. He was lying on his back on the doormat and sprawled on top of him was a small, furry creature with a face not unlike his own. It was brown, with shining brown eyes and a small nose that twitched. It had whiskers around the nose and little white teeth in its little mouth. It was puffing and blowing and shaking with excitement. Its nose was cold and wet and was pressed firmly against Snuff's own pink nose.

The creature spoke: "Oh dear! Oh, I am sorry!"

Snuff regarded the newcomer for some time and then said, slowly and calmly: "Well I never! You ought to be more careful, old fellow. I mean to say, accidents could happen…"

"I really am s-s-sorry" stuttered the newcomer. "I had no idea…that is, I didn't see…that is, I was in such a hurry…"

"Kindly allow me to get up," said Snuff, gently but firmly, for he was getting tired of conducting the conversation while lying on his back with the stranger spread out all over him.

"Oh, yes. I'm so s-s-sorry. I forgot. That is, I didn't realise…"

The furry intruder, still breathing heavily, clambered off Snuff and stood by rather sheepishly as Snuff rose to his feet with as much dignity as he could muster and brushed himself down with a careful paw.

Then he looked at his visitor again, from an upright position and with considerable interest.

"I don't seem to know you," he said. "Although, you are rather familiar looking. Are we related?"

The newcomer gazed around him, uncomfortably. "I'm sure I don't know, but I don't think so," he said, finally.

Snuff looked over the little creature again. "Well, you ARE a bit small, as rabbits go but…" Then he noticed something vital was missing.

"Where's your tail?" he asked, shocked.

The little stranger blinked in bewilderment.

"I'm not a rabbit," he said. "I'm a guinea pig and guinea pigs don't have…er, tails because, well, er, we d-d-don't need them."

"Guinea pig? Guinea pig? Never heard of such a thing!" exclaimed Snuff Rabbit, a trifle indignantly, because he did not like to have to admit not having heard of anything, let alone be confronted in his own house by something he had not heard of.

The guinea pig shivered and glanced over its shoulder, out through the open door. The poor animal looked thoroughly miserable.

"What's the matter?" asked Snuff, suddenly feeling rather sorry for his unexpected caller. "You can't be cold on a lovely evening like this."

"N-n-no, I'm not cold. I'm frightened, that's why I'm shivery. You s-s-see, I've escaped and THEY may be after me."

The guinea pig certainly spoke in a frightened way and kept looking over his shoulder, out of the still open door.

Snuff, now certain he had nothing to fear from the guinea pig, whatever a guinea pig might be, decided the time had come to display some hospitality, for which he was rightly famous throughout Jumbles Wood. He closed the door.

"Come into the parlour. THEY won't find you in here, whoever they might be. And you look as if a nice cup of cocoa would do you a bit of good."

He led the way down the passage into the parlour and waved his paw to indicate the most comfortable chair, close by the fireside.

"Sit down. Make yourself comfortable while I make the drink. A nice hot drink will make a new…er…guinea pig of you."

"Thank you" said the guinea pig, settling cautiously in the chair, his big eyes staring in wonder all around him. "My word, you have a lovely home here, don't you?"

"It suits me very nicely" called Snuff, from the scullery, rattling cups and saucers. "It's small, but it's warm and snug in the winter."

The guinea pig sighed. "It's like a palace," he said. "I've only ever lived in a cage."

CRASH! Snuff Rabbit dropped a cup in surprise. A cage? Whoever heard of anyone living in a cage. Who was this stranger he had invited into his home? A prisoner? He had said he had escaped – but where had he escaped from? Could it be…jail?

Snuff moved slowly back into the parlour.

Jumbles Wood

"WHERE did you say you had escaped from?" he inquired, as casually as he could.

The guinea pig looked up from the chair, where he was still perched on the edge as if frightened to relax.

"Why...er...from the Humans," he said.

CRASH! Snuff dropped another cup.

"Humans!" he gasped. "My dear fellow. My poor chap. No wonder you look worn out. You must have been running for miles. You must have been a fugitive for weeks. You should have said before! My, poor, dear chap!"

The guinea pig shifted uncomfortably on the edge of the chair.

"Well, n-n-not exactly. I've been on the run for, about, er, half-an-hour."

Snuff Rabbit was not holding a cup now, which was perhaps as well, for had he been, he may well have dropped a third to join the shattered remnants of the other two. For the little, shivering, pathetic looking guinea pig was providing him with shock after shock.

All the creatures of Jumbles Wood knew about Humans, of course. Some had even had some dealings with them. But all knew that the nearest Humans lived miles and miles away and never came near Jumbles Wood. Snuff knew this as well as most and, gazing at the Guinea Pig's short, stubby legs, he wondered how the poor creature could have run so many miles in only half-an-hour.

"Look here, old chap," he began awkwardly, eyeing the little short legs, "I don't want to appear personal, and all that, but you don't look as if you could run all that fast. I mean to say, the nearest Humans must be about seven miles away, if not more."

"One and-a-half miles," said the guinea pig, abruptly and with a firmness that indicated he was absolutely sure. "I know I'm not much of a runner over long distances. I'm just not built for it. But I'm good at estimating distances and it's no more than a mile and-a-half to the big red house."

"Big red house?" repeated Snuff, incredulously. "I don't know of any big red house. I've seen the nearest Human house to Jumbles Wood – my father took me to see it when I was little more than a boy – but that house was white, with ivy growing on the walls.

"It was north of here and my father told me it was a place to keep away from in case there were dogs."

Jumbles Wood

The guinea pig nodded. "I've come from the north," he agreed. "But the Humans I escaped from lived in a big red house and it was only a mile and-a-half away. It's a new house and what's more, another one is being built next to it."

"Oh My Goodness!" exclaimed Snuff, in alarm. "Only a mile and-a-half! Humans living that near. This is terrible – I'll have to move."

Then his eyes widened as another thought struck him. It wasn't just his little house that was near to the new Human house – it was the whole of Jumbles Wood. The thought of leaving Snuff's Oak was bad enough, but the thought of the whole of Jumbles Wood being deserted by its animal inhabitants was…well, it was unthinkable!

He looked again at the guinea pig. He noted his muddy paws, his general bedraggled appearance and his heavy breathing. There could be no doubt about the truth of his story. He had obviously been on the run and was clearly badly frightened.

And with those little legs, he could not possibly have travelled far, no matter how much of a panic he had been in.

The matter had to be faced squarely. Jumbles Wood was threatened by Humans.

Snuff looked again at his shivery visitor.

"I'll get you that drink I promised you," he said.

"Thanks, v-v-very much," stuttered the guinea pig.

Over two steaming mugs of cocoa and in front of a blazing fire, which Snuff built up as the cold of the night began to make itself felt, the two animals talked.

"I've never had a chance, what with all the shocks I have been having, to ask you your name, said Snuff.

The guinea pig wriggled uncomfortably and replied: "It's…er…Hammy."

"Hammy? Well, I once knew a hamster of that name, but…"

"Yes, I know," interrupted the guinea pig, before Snuff could say any more. "You see, I was given my name by the Humans. They bought me from what they call a pet shop, and they thought I was a hamster. When they found out I was really a guinea pig they couldn't stop calling me Hammy."

"They must have been very stupid," observed Snuff.

"Yes, they were, about animals. They thought I would be happy living in a little cage in the garden."

Snuff was puzzled. "I have heard," he said, "that Humans sometimes keep rabbits in cages. I can't understand it. You say they wanted you to be happy, but at the same time they kept you a prisoner."

Hammy sighed. "It is strange. They didn't think I was a prisoner. They said I was a pet. The grown-up Humans gave me plenty to eat and drink and their little boy and little girl played with me – particularly the little girl. But I didn't really like being their pet. Eventually, I managed to escape by squeezing through the wires of the cage."

He shivered. "I expect they are out looking for me now."

The two animals listened, but outside Snuff's snug little house they could hear nothing but the soft murmur of the wind, the rustle of leaves and the occasional patter of feet as some night creature went passed on his own business.

"Perhaps they won't miss you until morning," suggested Snuff. "Perhaps they won't bother looking for you at all."

"I think they will. The boy and girl will, anyway, because in their own funny way they were fond of me. I suppose it isn't their fault that they don't know that animals don't like being kept in cages."

The two animals sat by the fire late into the night, discussing the arrival of the Humans. They talked of many things, thought of many plans but, in the end, only came to one definite decision.

A special emergency meeting must be called of all the animals of Jumbles Wood.

CHAPTER 2

Spreading the word

The rattling of milk bottles aroused Snuff Rabbit from a deep, deep sleep, in which he had been dreaming he was being chased by Humans and had lost his voice and couldn't call for help. It had been almost dawn when he and Hammy the guinea pig had eventually gone to bed, so he had only had a few hours sleep and was still tired.

But the rattling of the milk bottles awakened him, for he knew it was important that he speak with Blink Otter. Who better than the milkman to spread the word about the Humans?

He dashed to the front door and flung it open just as Blink was bending to pick up his empty bottles.

"By Jimminy!" exclaimed the startled otter, blinking at Snuff. "You did give me a turn, Snuff Rabbit. It's not often I see anyone awake this early in the morning."

Blink Otter was always blinking at people. That was how he had got his name. But when he was surprised, he blinked even more than usual.

He looked curiously at the excited, but rather bleary-eyed rabbit. "What's the matter? You look as if you have been up all night."

"I have. At least I've been up nearly all night, which is just as bad. Blink Otter, you have important work to do this morning."

Blink pushed out his chest with pride. "I know that," he said. "My work is important every morning. I make sure that all Jumbles Wood gets milk – and that's very important. Milk is very good for you. It gives you energy."

"Yes, yes, I know all that," said Snuff impatiently. "But you've got even more important work to do today, as well as delivering milk. You have a message to give to every one of your customers."

Swiftly, he told the otter of the events of the previous night. As he spoke, Blink blinked more and more and with ever increasing speed until his eyelids began to ache.

"Humans – less than two miles from here," he gasped. "Good Grief! There's a family of badgers live out that way and I've delivered milk to them this morning. The Human house must be very close to them, but I'm sure they don't know anything about it."

"We must call a meeting this very day," said Snuff. "Pass the word that all animals should assemble outside my house at noon."

Blink Otter nodded. "Leave it to me. I know my duty. I'll spread the word. Jumbles Wood expects every fellow to do his duty."

And off he went, banging loudly on every door, instead of simply leaving the milk as he normally did.

"Human's threaten Jumbles Wood! Emergency meeting at Snuff's Oak at noon!" he bellowed through each letter box. And the inhabitants of the woodland community leapt from their beds in alarm as the warning message spread.

Old Crow, who, in his own opinion at least, was the most important creature in Jumbles Wood, was wide awake and having breakfast, high in his house on Crow's Nest Hill, when Blink Otter arrived, panting and hoarse.

The wily old bird was always an early riser and was invariably irritable by the time Blink arrived because he had been kept waiting for his milk. This morning Blink was later than usual, because of having to stop and tell everyone about the Humans, so Old Crow was in an even more vile mood than was customary.

Old Crow was actually a jackdaw – possibly the liveliest member of the crow family. He had earned his name by becoming the oldest crow in Jumbles Wood – and self-appointed leader of all the crows, jackdaws and rooks in the wood.

He glared down from his house, in a crevice in a birch tree, as he saw the out-of-breath otter arriving.

"You may well pant and puff, you blinking otter," he called down. "Why is my milk so late?"

Blink blinked up at him. "Old Crow – you'll never guess. I have an important message."

"Have you got my milk?" cackled the jackdaw, angrily. "That's what's important to me this morning."

"No…that is, yes," stammered Blink, who like most folk in Jumbles Wood, was just a little afraid of the crow's sharp tongue.

Flapping his wings, Old Crow fluttered down to the ground and clawed at the milk bottles Blink Otter was holding. "Gimme, gimme!" he rasped.

"Old Crow – there are Humans living only a mile and-a-half away and there's an emergency meeting at Snuff's Oak at noon," said Blink, hurriedly, so that his angry customer couldn't interrupt him again.

"Gimme that milk" cackled Old Crow. "Gimme that….eh? What? What did you say?"

Blink blinked, rather more importantly as he gained confidence and repeated the message. "Humans have built a house only a mile and-a-half to the north of Jumbles Wood and Snuff Rabbit has called an emergency meeting at his place at noon."

Old Crow's fury abated for a moment. "Humans," he said, quite softly. "Humans, eh? Well I knew it would happen. I always knew it."

Then he became angry again. "Snuff Rabbit! Snuff Rabbit has called a meeting? Who does he think he is, eh? What business is it of his to call a meeting?"

"Well, er, it was Snuff who found out about it first, I think," said Blink, blinking nervously.

"What's needed is a keen mind and a cool head," Old Crow said. "We need somebody of authority. Someone with personality, ability and a razor sharp mind. We need somebody with energy, foresight and wisdom. That's who we need to take charge in a situation like this."

"Have you someone in mind" asked, Blink, knowing what the answer would be.

"Of course I have, you silly otter. There's only one person for the job. Me!"

Blink nodded vigorously, not so much because he agreed with Old Crow, but because he thought it better to appear to agree.

Jumbles Wood

"Well, er, the meeting is at Snuff's Oak and half Jumbles Wood knows about it already," he said. "You'd better go and take charge there. I've got to get on my way so everybody will get to know about it."

Blink hurried off, leaving Old Crow standing at the foot of the birch muttering away about foresight, wisdom, energy and such like.

All through Jumbles Wood, Blink went calling on badgers, rabbits, squirrels, hares, mice, voles, birds of various types and, indeed, all the furry and feathery inhabitants. An hour before noon he had completed his round, exhausted his supply of milk and energy and repeated his story so many times that he had almost lost his voice. He pushed his little cart back to his dairy, on the banks of Deep River and then set off for the meeting.

CHAPTER 3

A little friend lost

Amanda awoke to find early morning sunlight shining through her bedroom curtains.

Getting up in the morning had become a wonderful thing since they came to live in the countryside, she thought. Even on school days!

Father had been right. When he told them all he was going to build them a new house out in the countryside, away from the noisy town with its factories and smoking chimneys, she had been worried. It would mean moving to a new school, leaving all her friends behind her and starting a new life.

Her brother Robin had not been at all bothered. He had liked the idea of living out in the fields, near to a big wood and a river where he would be able to go fishing with Father.

Mother had been a bit strange. She liked the idea of living in the countryside but, she had told them all, she didn't like the idea of building a new house.

"New houses spoil the country," she said. "Can't we find a house that is already there?"

But father had explained that he had found a field that had planning permission for several houses.

"If we don't build them, someone else will," he said. "I don't want to spoil the countryside either, so I will build nice houses that won't spoil it."

So Father, who owned a building company, had built the house, which they decided to call Green Slates, not far from the village of Green Valley and quite close to Jumbles Wood, near a bend in Deep River where there were no other houses. And they had moved – and Amanda had to admit, everything seemed perfect.

Now Father was starting to build the other houses.

Amanda heard her mother calling: "I won't tell you again, Amanda Watson. It's time to get up." She knew that when she got her name in full, Mother was serious. It really was time to get up.

The house was a noisy place first thing in the morning with herself and Robin fighting over the bathroom and Mother and Father getting breakfast ready.

Robin's first job of the day was to go out and make sure his dog, Max, was all right while Amanda had to give her guinea pig his breakfast.

Max had been a member of the family for several years but, being rather a large Alsatian, lived in a kennel in the garden. The guinea pig was called Hammy – something which Amanda was rather embarrassed about. She had gone with her Mother to buy a hamster from a pet shop, but neither of them knew the difference between a hamster and a guinea pig and both of them had got used to calling him Hammy before they found out they had made a mistake.

But she loved the little animal dearly and he seemed to suit his name.

Robin and Father thought it was a huge joke – but they were all very fond of Hammy.

Amanda got the box of special guinea pig food and went out to his hutch.

Moments later she was running back into the house.

"Mum! Dad! Hammy's gone!" she cried.

Mother looked up from the worktop where she was preparing packed lunches for Amanda and Robin to take to school.

"Gone? What do you mean, gone?"

"There's a hole in the cage – and he's gone," screamed Amanda.

"I'll take a look," said Father.

He went out into the garden, followed by the two children.

Sure enough, the wire netting at the front of the hutch and been forced forward to leave a small hole – and the hutch was empty.

"Well, I'll be blowed," said Father, scratching his head. "How could he have done that?"

"He must be stronger than he looks," said Robin.

Amanda was sobbing now. Her eyes filled with tears and she began to run around the garden calling "Hammy, Hammy, where are you?"

Robin was searching among the bushes. The guinea pig was not his pet, but he knew how much his sister loved the little animal. He also knew how he would feel if Max were to disappear.

"Don't cry, Mandy," he said. "He can't have gone far. He's probably here in the garden somewhere. I can't see how he could get through the fence."

Father said: "You're quite right, Robin. He'll be here somewhere. But we haven't got time to look for him now. You two have got to get off to school. I'll have a look round to see if I can find him after you have gone."

"But, Dad...." Amanda began. She was fighting back tears – but not very successfully.

"No buts, Mandy. You must go to school. I promise I will look for him as soon as you have gone. He'll probably be back in his hutch when you get back tonight."

Amanda wanted to argue, but she knew she would be wasting her time. Once her father had made up his mind, he would not be changing it. He had decided they had to go to school and that was that. In any case, she knew it was important not to miss school.

As Mother drove them off in her car Amanda looked back over her shoulder and saw Father looking behind the tool shed, so at least she knew he was keeping his word. Probably, Hammy would be back in his hutch when she returned home.

Harry Watson started searching the garden yard by yard. He had an important 'phone call to make to a builder's merchant about an order for thousands of bricks. He did not have much time. But he knew his daughter would be devastated if her guinea pig was not found. The 'phone call would have to wait.

Amanda found it difficult to concentrate on her lessons that day. Once or twice the teacher had to reprimand her for staring out of the classroom window instead of paying attention. The day seemed to last much longer than usual.

At lunch time, all she wanted to talk about was the missing guinea pig. Some of her friends just laughed, others were more sympathetic. But, somehow, even the kind ones only made her feel worse when they kept saying: "Every thing will be all right he'll be there when you get home."

When the bell rang for the end of the last lesson of the day, she was among the first out of the classroom and on the car park. Robin was only moments behind her, but there was no sign of Mother's car.

They had to wait a few minutes as other parents drove up, collected children and drove away - minutes which to Amanda seemed to last for hours.

Then the car appeared at the school entrance…and Amanda's heart sank. The look on her mother's face told her what she had dreaded all day. Hammy was still missing.

Mother got out of the car and said, simply: "I'm sorry, dear. We haven't found him. Your Dad is still looking and we've asked all the men on the building site to keep an eye open for him too. But no-one has seen a sign of him."

Amanda could no longer hold back the tears. She banged her hands on the car bonnet and started to sob uncontrollably.

The teacher saw what was happening and hurried across the car park. "What's is the matter, Mandy – it's not like you to cry and be so unhappy."

She turned to Mother and added: "Mandy's not been her usual self today, Mrs Watson. Something seems to be bothering her. She's not been concentrating at all well."

Mother explained and the teacher gave Amanda a little hug. "Don't worry," she said. "He'll turn up."

"That's what everyone says," wailed Amanda. "But he won't, I know he won't."

She managed, briefly, to stop herself from crying until the car pulled away but then sobbed all the way home.

"Good Heavens!" said Robin. "How long are we going to have to put up with this?"

"Don't be unkind," said Mother. "You know how much she loves Hammy. We've all got to try and help her."

"The only way you can help is to find him," sobbed Amanda.

CHAPTER 4

The emergency meeting

Close by Snuff's Oak there was a grassy clearing among the trees where toadstools and wild flowers grew in the spring and summer. It was a place where the animals sometimes held fairs or sports days and it was, thought Snuff Rabbit, the idea place for the emergency meeting.

Hammy, the Guinea Pig, had slept late after his ordeal of the night before, but when he eventually awoke he tucked into a good breakfast of porridge, toast and marmalade and hot coffee. He helped Snuff carry out a large desk which they placed at one end of the clearing. The desk had belonged to Snuff's great, great grandfather and was made of old, dark brown wood. It had beautifully carved legs and brass handles on the drawers and was most impressive. Snuff thought it would be just the thing from which to address the meeting.

Blink Otter was first to arrive, footsore and weary after his rounds.

"I've told everybody – I think there will be a good attendance," he said.

"There had better be, " said Snuff. "This is probably the most important meeting ever to be held in Jumbles Wood."

He pointed to the desk, which stood on a slight rise.

"I thought I'd address the gathering from there," he explained. "I'll give a short outline of the situation as I see it and then introduce Hammy – Oh, Blink, you've not met Hammy have you?

"Blink, this is Hammy. Hammy, this is Blink."

Jumbles Wood

Snuff chattered on while Hammy and Blink shook paws and said: "How do you do?" to each other.

"Hammy is the one who actually discovered the Humans, you know. In fact, he was their prisoner until he escaped," said the rabbit.

Blink was impressed. Anyone who could escape from Humans was indeed a clever fellow.

"Tell me," he asked, "Why are you called Hammy when you are not a hamster?"

Hammy explained. He also explained that he was a Guinea Pig and that he wasn't supposed to have a tail. And all the time, Snuff chattered away in the background about his plans for the meeting.

Eventually he turned to Blink and asked: "Do you think it will be all right?"

"Will what be all right?" enquired Blink, who was still marvelling over the fact that Guinea Pigs could look so like rabbits and yet manage without a tail.

"Why, the meeting of course, you silly otter!"

"Oh, yes." Blink regarded his friend for a moment and then said, cautiously: "You may…er…have a little trouble at the meeting. You might find that somebody else has a few ideas about how it should be organised…"

Snuff waited while Blink paused in mid-sentence, for maximum effect.

"Old Crow," said Blink, as if nothing else needed to be said. And it didn't, for Snuff knew at once what he meant.

"Ah! Old Crow thinks he should organise the meeting?"

Blink nodded. "Precisely. In fact, he seems rather annoyed that you have arranged the meeting at all. He seems to think it's his job."

Snuff sighed. "I might have known it. That's the trouble with Old Crow. He means well, but…well, you know!"

"Yes, I know," said Blink. "But Old Crow says we need someone with a keen brain, great wisdom, energy and foresight to take charge of the situation."

Hammy nodded eagerly. "I don't know this Old Crow, of course. But I agree with him. If anything is to be done about the Humans, we shall need wisdom, energy and a great deal more too. Who does Old Crow have in mind?"

Snuff and Blink looked at each other and then at Hammy.

"You certainly don't know Old Crow," said Snuff, smiling in spite of himself. "Old Crow only knows one person with wisdom, energy, foresight and all the rest. And that's Old Crow himself!"

"Oh dear! He sounds awfully conceited," said Hammy in dismay. "Can he really be trusted with such responsibility if he thinks like that?"

Snuff looked wistfully at the desk, where he had fondly imagined himself standing addressing the entire population of Jumbles Wood.

"You can trust him to make sure he takes charge of the meeting, and that's for sure," he said. "Old Crow is very good at taking charge."

A dark shadow swooped over the clearing and a sharp voice said: "Old Crow is very good at most things."

The three animals started in surprise as the black bird settled next to them.

"Oh, hello Old Crow," said Snuff, recovering quickly. "We were just talking about you."

"So I heard" said Old Crow. He eyed Hammy curiously. "And who is this, might I enquire?"

Snuff said: "This is Hammy. He's the one who found out about the Humans first. He was their prisoner, but he escaped."

"I'm pleased to meet you, I'm sure," said Hammy.

Old Crow nodded curtly. "A guinea pig, eh? Well, that's something new for Jumbles Wood."

Blink Otter blinked. "You KNOW what he is?" he said in surprise.

"There's not much I don't know," said Old Crow. He produced a large book from under his wing and began leafing through the pages. "I always carry a dictionary – you never know when it might come in useful. Ah! Here we are, let me see."

He pointed a claw at one of the pages and began to read: "Guinea Pig. Native of South America. Name taken from the Guinana pig. Rodent. Often kept as pets by Humans." He paused and stared at Hammy's furry rear end and added: "No tail."

Hammy looked embarrassed. "I don't know anything about that," he said. "I don't even know where South America is. I can't remember being anywhere before the pet shop."

"Take my word for it," said Old Crow, briskly. "Now, to more important things. I see you have a desk ready for me to address the meeting. Yes, very good. I think you've put it in the correct place."

Snuff took a deep breath to help him control his temper. Old Crow's conceit was just too much.

"Well, thank you very much, I'm sure," he said. "Actually, I thought Hammy and I would address the meeting.

"I will open the proceedings and then introduce Hammy who, having actually been at the Human's house and having actually lived with the Humans, must know more about them then any of us."

Old Crow fixed a beady eye on Snuff. "I agree," he said, slowly, "that our friend the guinea pig must be considered an important witness of the arrival of the Humans. But what, Snuff Rabbit, do you know about the situation, other than what you have been told by others?"

"W-w-why, nothing!" admitted Snuff.

"Then I shall take the chair," cackled the crow in triumph.

Snuff was not giving up as easily as that. Nearly everyone in Jumbles Wood was a little afraid of Old Crow and Snuff was no exception. But circumstances had made him, Snuff Rabbit, an important figure in the affair of the Humans and he did not see why he should be pushed aside by the arrogant bird.

"Well, Old Crow," he replied, sharply. "Just what knowledge of the Humans do you have, other than what you have been told by others?"

Old Crow flapped his wings impatiently. "Let's not be childish, Snuff Rabbit. Do you think I have been sitting idly in my house all morning? Why the first thing I did after receiving the news from Blink Otter was to go and see the Human house for myself.

"I flew over it for a whole hour, studying the house and the surrounding land which the Humans have fenced in. Why, I probably know more about it than our friend Hammy here."

Jumbles Wood

Snuff was beaten. The crafty Old Crow had moved swiftly to make sure he could not be ignored. It was true that having flown over the house, the bad tempered bird must be considered an expert on the subject of the Humans.

All Snuff could say, rather lamely, was: "Well…it IS my desk."

"Very well," said Old Crow. "I shall take the chair, but you can be on the platform too. And Hammy, of course."

Old Crow paused and turned his piercing gaze on Hammy.

"Incidentally, how on earth does a Guinea Pig come to be called Hammy?" he enquired sharply. Hammy sighed and told the story.

"Hah! Typical! Humans can be very stupid," said the crow. "Well, let's get on. People should be turning up for the meeting soon."

"Ah-hum!" said Blink Otter, loudly. They all turned to look at him as he stood there, paws behind his back, rocking backwards and forwards on his heels and blinking furiously.

"Did you say something, Blink Otter?" asked Old Crow, crossly.

"Ah-hum! Yes I…er..did."

"Well then speak up. What do you want to say?"

Blink hesitated and then said, all of a rush: "Well, seeing as I have told everyone in Jumbles Wood about the Humans, don't you think I ought to be on the platform too?"

Old Crow spread his wings in annoyance.

"Good Grief. Everybody wants to be in on the act. Well, all right. I don't see why not, as long as you don't expect to say anything."

"Oh, I don't want to say anything," smiled Blink, happily. "It's just that…well…I mean…well I DID spread the word, didn't I?"

When the animals of Jumbles Wood began to arrive for the emergency meeting at the clearing near Snuff's Oak, they found a party of four waiting impatiently at the big desk. Old Crow and Snuff were in the middle, Blink Otter was on the left and Hammy the Guinea Pig was on the right.

The animals came from far and wide. There were otters and water rats from Deep River, badgers from the old sand quarry that lay in the shadow of Crow's Nest Hill. There were voles and mice, squirrels, moles and weasels and stoats. There were rooks, magpies and sparrows.   Just about every creature you could think of. And they all gathered before the big desk, with its carved legs and brass handles.

Old Crow, having got his own way about who should be chairman, relented somewhat. His closest friends knew that although his tongue was sharp, he was really quite soft when you got to know him.

After briefly explaining the reason why the meeting had been called, he asked Snuff to introduce Hammy. Snuff said a few words and then Hammy, a little nervously in front of such a big crowd of strangers, told of his escape from the Humans.

Old Crow then described how he had flown over the Human's house, observed two adult Humans, a small boy and small girl and a large dog. He also reported signs of another house being built – possibly more than one. All the time, the assembled birds and animals listened intently.

"The question is," said Old Crow, finally, "What can we do about these Humans? Or, indeed, is there anything we can do about them?"

He was answered only by a hushed silence.

"Well, come on now. Has anyone any suggestions or questions?"

A small hamster jumped up. "I have a question," he piped.

"Let's have it then," said Old Crow, briskly.

"What I would like to know is…" the hamster paused…"Why is a guinea pig called Hammy?"

Old Crow groaned. Blink Otter blinked. Snuff Rabbit wiggled his ears in annoyance and Hammy blushed to the tips of his whiskers.

A great hoot of derision came from the crowd when Snuff explained how the guinea pig had got his name. An old, grey badger stood up and motioned for silence.

"If the Humans are that stupid, we ought to be able to do something about them, " he said. "They are obviously not very bright."

The badger rubbed his eyes, scratched his head thoughtfully for a second or two and then sat down again.

An otter raised a paw. "I have a question too. Why don't guinea pigs have tails?"

Hammy blushed again, but Old Crow came to his rescue.

"This is ridiculous," he shouted. "Here we are, facing perhaps the biggest threat to Jumbles Wood there ever has been, and all you can think of are stupid questions about our friend Hammy. Don't you realise he has given us a chance to save ourselves?

"Jumbles Wood may be threatened with INVASION! We may ALL be taken prisoner like Hammy was. If we manage to think of a way of saving ourselves, we shall have Hammy to thank for bringing us an early warning."

There was a long silence. The animals felt ashamed, especially the hamster and the otter who had asked questions about the newcomer in their midst.

Finally the badger said doubtfully: "There MUST he something we can do."

Old Crow flapped his wings. "Of course there must. But it's no good just repeating yourself, you silly old badger. We must act. We must think."

The badger ignored Old Crow's insult. He was old and no longer worried about things like that. There was a time when he would have challenged Old Crow for leadership of the animal community, but now he was content to live peacefully and quietly. He did not really want to bother his tired old mind with problems and worries.

"In the old days," he said, "We would have had an Animal's Council to deal with problems like this."

"An Animal's Council? What's that?" asked Snuff Rabbit.

The badger fumbled in his fur, found an itch and scratched it slowly and carefully before answering. Old Crow impatiently tapped a claw on the desk while everyone waited.

Finally the badger spoke again. "Well, it's clear that the problem of the Humans cannot be solved overnight. It's going to take a lot of thought and a lot of planning. We can't keep calling all the animals of Jumbles Wood together every time some decision has to be taken. We need a small group of organisers to do the day-to-day work. That's an Animal Council."

Old Crow flapped his wings in agreement. "You are quite right, old fellow. We must elect a Council at once."

The badger found another itch and scratched it just as slowly and carefully as he had scratched the first one.

"I propose," he said slowly, "that seeing as the four folk on the platform here today have made such a good job of organising this meeting, they should be the Council."

"I second that," snapped Old Crow, forgetting for a moment that really he should have left it to some other person from the general assembly to do the seconding.

"Everyone in favour put up their paw, claw or wing," he added hurriedly.

A forest of arms went up as the animals, glad to be relieved of the responsibility of deciding what to do next, voted for the four members of the platform party.

"Thank you for that vote of confidence in us," said Old Crow, warming to the task of being chairman. "I'm sure it will not be misplaced."

The old badger raised a paw. "There remains one more point to settle," he said, slowly, ignoring the beady stare he was getting from Old Crow. "I think the Council should have a leader – someone to take full responsibility for the taking of decisions in an emergency."

Old Crow puffed out his chest, importantly. "I agree entirely," he piped.

Snuff Rabbit stepped forward.

"I agree too," he said. "We need somebody of authority. Someone with personality, ability and a razor sharp mind."

Old Crow nodded and cried: "Hear, hear."

"We need somebody with energy," Snuff went on. "And foresight and wisdom. That's who we need to take charge in a situation like this."

"I couldn't agree more," cackled Old Crow, his chest bulging with pride. "You are speaking good sense, Snuff Rabbit, and I shall be only too pleased to..."

But Snuff hadn't finished yet.

"We need somebody with military experience," he ended, firmly.

"Eh? What are you talking about? I haven't any military experience," snapped Old Crow, impatiently.

"No," said Snuff. "But Brigadier Fox has."

A hush fell on the clearing. You could have heard a leaf fall from one the trees. Even Old Crow was, for once, speechless.

Jumbles Wood

Finally he croaked feebly: "B-b-brigadier Fox?"

"Yes," said Snuff. "This is a state of war we find ourselves in. Jumbles Wood   is threatened with invasion and we should put ourselves on a war footing. And Brigadier Fox is the only person I know with any experience of military command."

The hush continued, getting ever quieter, if that was possible. Every creature in the clearing knew of Brigadier Fox. No animal in Jumbles Wood was better known. Yet none counted him as a friend, few even as an acquaintance. Most feared him.

Even in the present emergency, Blink Otter had not spread the news to Brigadier Fox.

The wily old fox lived on his own in a part of Jumbles Wood that was seldom visited by any but the bravest of animals. Just where he had acquired his military rank, no-one knew and none had ever dared inquire.

A brass plate outside his door stated in bold letters "Brig. R.E.D. Fox, JWA (Rtd)" but nobody really knew what it meant – not even Old Crow.

It was said that in his younger days, Brigadier Fox had chased other animals and had been rather partial to rabbit pie. But again, none could really say. Everybody kept out of his way.

The hush in the clearing continued for what seemed a long time, until eventually the old badger said: "I don't see Brigadier Fox here today."

Blink Otter rose to his feet, blinking. "I…I didn't get as far as his house. He doesn't know about the meeting."

"No he doesn't," said Snuff Rabbit. "And that means he doesn't know about the Humans either. I think he would help us."

"Nonsense, nonsense," cackled Old Crow. "This is ridiculous. We all know about Brigadier Fox. We've kept away from him for years because he's our enemy. Why should we now think he would be our friend?

"We might just as well go and ask the Green Wizard for help."

If it were possible, the silence grew more silent. The mention of Brigadier Fox had shocked everyone present, except Snuff, who had done the mentioning, and possibly the old badger, who didn't seem to be shocked by anything. But the mention of the Green Wizard seemed to startled even him.

Jumbles Wood

Blink Otter, blinking even more than ever, said: "The G-G-Green W-W-Wizard is a Human himself – we can't expect help from him."

Old Crow was rather pleased with himself. By bringing up the subject of the Wizard he had made everyone forget Brigadier Fox. And, in his opinion, at least, that meant there was only one other person to be leader. Old Crow himself!

He flapped his wings airily. "I know he is a Human," said. "But he chooses to live here in Jumbles Wood with us."

Snuff Rabbit said thoughtfully: "He never has anything to do with us. I don't think any animal has ever been near him."

"No – but that is because we won't go near him," said Old Crow.

But Snuff went on: "The Wizard never has anything to do with anyone – animal or Human. He just seems to want to live by himself in that old cave of his. But he might be willing to help us."

The old badger had been listening to what was said calmly. He raised a paw and spoke again.

"We know nothing about the Wizard, except that he has lived in Jumbles Wood for a long, long time and spends most of his time boiling strange smelling potions in a big pot outside his cave.

"He has never done harm to any animal, so far as we know. He eats only berries from the trees and roots from the ground. He does not set traps for animals, as some Humans do.

"But he has nothing to do with us. We don't even know if he would understand us if we went to see him. And, as Blink Otter says, he is a HUMAN. If we are at war with Humans he is surely more likely to be on their side.

"Brigadier Fox, on the other hand, is very much a creature of the woods. He is an animal like ourselves.

"I know him better than most. He and I are…well, not exactly friends, but…well, we have an understanding. We are among the oldest inhabitants of Jumbles Wood and we respect each other's way of life.

"I know he has a bad reputation among many of you and that most of you are afraid of him because of this. But Brigadier Fox has his own enemies and the worst of these are the Humans and their dogs. I think that if Jumbles

Wood is threatened by the Humans then Brigadier Fox will be as concerned as any of us. I think he will help us if we ask him."

"That's just it – who's going to ask him?" cackled Old Crow, annoyed that talk had got back to the fox.

"I will," said Snuff, abruptly.

"And I w-w-will g-g-go with you," piped the small voice of Hammy.

"Ha!" laughed Old Crow. "A rabbit and a guinea pig going to see a fox. I've never heard of anything so ridiculous."

Blink Otter rose to his feet, blinking. "I will go too," he said.

Every eye turned on Old Crow. He was now the only member of the newly-elected Council who had not volunteered to go and see Brigadier Fox.

For a long time there was a silence and then he shrugged his black shoulders and flapped his wings impatiently.

"Very well," he snapped. "I agree. I too shall go and see the Brigadier. But I don't hold out much hope of help from him."

A general murmur of approval came from the assembly.

Old Crow, rapidly recovering his confidence now that he made his decision, called above the noise: "That's all now, folks. We shall call another meeting if necessary and in the meantime, Blink Otter will continue to spread the word if there is any news. We shall count on you all for your assistance in this time of...er...national crisis."

The crotchety old Jackdaw was rather pleased with having said that. It was not everybody, he thought, who could think up things like "time of national crisis". He had been having rather a rough time of it during the meeting. That final, flowing phrase had restored his position of authority, he felt. All he needed now was for Brigadier Fox to refuse to help and...well he could already see himself being made Commander in Chief.

All the animals began to move off and soon the clearing was empty except for the four members of the new Animal's Council, standing behind the big wooden desk. Suddenly it seemed very quiet and the woods around seemed very still. The size of the problems facing them began to weigh down upon them.

And the prospect of a visit to Brigadier Fox's house didn't help matters at all.

"Well," said Snuff. "When had we better go and see the Brigadier?"

Old Crow laughed dryly.

"Getting cold feet?" he inquired, in a sarcastic voice. "I mean, it was YOUR idea, Snuff Rabbit."

Snuff nodded. "I know," he said. "It's just that, well, it's getting late in the day, isn't it?"

"Nonsense! The day is young." Old Crow was enjoying himself again.

Hammy chipped in. "It is a national crisis," he said. "I don't think we can afford to waste time. The sooner we go to see this Brigadier Fox, the sooner we will know if he will help us."

"It's all right for you," said Blink Otter. "You don't know him."

"Well," said Old Crow, "We have promised to go, so go we must. And I agree with Hammy. The sooner the better. Let's get this desk back in your house, Snuff Rabbit, and then we'll be off."

And so it was that the four animals set off across Jumbles Wood to visit the home of Brigadier R.E.D. Fox, JWA. (Rtd) – whatever all that meant.

CHAPTER 5

Appointment with fear

Brigadier Fox lived in the most thickly wooded part of Jumbles Wood and to reach his home, the four friends had to make their way along narrow, winding paths that were nearly overgrown through lack of use. Prickly thorns and stinging nettles lined each side of the path and overhead the branches of great trees, oak, elm, beech and birch, formed a lattice work through which only a little daylight could penetrate.

As they walked, Snuff, Hammy and Blink could hear only the sound of their own feet and the flutter of Old Crow's wings as he hovered above their heads, for it seemed that no breath of wind could reach this dark part of Jumbles Wood to stir a leaf or twig, and no bird sang. It was all very spooky.

"I d-d-don't like it," stammered Hammy, and his voice sounded loud and yet strangely muffled in all that silence. "I've lived all my life with Humans, who are always bustling about and making a noise. I didn't like being a prisoner in a cage, but I never felt so f-frightened as I do now."

Blink Otter lived most of his life within earshot of the tinkling waters of Deep River and he was also used to the rattling of milk bottles around his little dairy.

"I don't like it either," he said. "It's so quiet and…spooky."

Snuff Rabbit was used to silence, for of a night in his underground parlour the only sound was the ticking of his grandfather clock. But he didn't like the strange stillness of this black forest either.

Old Crow said nothing, for although he felt uneasy, he believed he had to set an example of leadership. He could not afford to appear to be afraid.

He would have loved to have been soaring high in the sunlight, with a fresh wind blowing through his feathers. He could, of course, have flown above the trees and met the other three when they reached Brigadier Fox's house. But he felt it his duty to stay with the them.

It seemed they travelled for hours and by the time they neared their destination there were three pairs of aching feet and one pair of tired wings in the party.

"I hope we've not wasted our time," said Old Crow. "We mustn't forget that this part of Jumbles Wood is much further from the Human house than where we live. Brigadier Fox may not be bothered about them, they are so far from his house."

Snuff said: "It's our job to persuade him that he is as much in danger as the rest of us. Anyway, these Humans can travel so much faster than us, in their cars, that the whole of Jumbles Wood is within easy reach of that house."

The four friends fell silent as they approached the big house where Brigadier Fox lived. Like Snuff's home, it was underground, beneath a giant oak tree. But somehow it looked much more imposing.

They stopped at the door and eyed the imposing brass plate. They looked at each other uneasily. They looked at the large brass knocker on the heavy oak door. And they said nothing.

Finally Blink Otter took a deep breath and said: "W-well, somebody had better knock."

"Go on then," snapped Old Crow. "You're the tallest. You can reach the knocker best."

Blink regarded the bird in his usual blinking way. He thought of pointing out that Old Crow, as the only flying fellow present, could reach the knocker even more easily than he. But then he realised it would only lead to an argument.

So he stepped resolutely forward, stood on tip-toe and grasped the big knocker.

Tap, tap, tap.

"Good Grief," exclaimed Old Crow. "He'll never hear that. Knock louder!"

Blink stood on his toes again, grasped the knocker and was just about to knock with all his strength when, suddenly, the door was flung open from within. The surprised otter had no time to let go of the knocker and as a result was hurled, headlong, through the door and sprawled full length on the floor inside.

"Yaaaa-hoooooo!" he howled in terror.

"Great Scott!" exclaimed Old Crow, flapping his wings so fiercely that he rose a full three feet off the ground.

Snuff and Hammy were speechless and for a moment there was no sound from either side of the door.

Then a sharp and piercing voice exclaimed: "Blistering bombshells! What's this? What d'you think you are doin' sir?

Brigadier Fox, resplendent in scarlet uniform and peaked cap, stood inside the door, staring in amazement at the prostrate otter in his hall.

"I...I...that is, we....well!" stuttered Blink, blinking furiously.

Old Crow came down to earth with a bump and the Brigadier suddenly became aware of the fact that he had more than one visitor.

"What...what ...what is the meanin' of this?" he rapped, in brisk, military style.

"We're sorry to trouble you, sir," began Snuff, stepping forward.

"But we have come to you for help," added Hammy.

"We have important news," piped Old Crow, regaining some of his poise and pomposity.

"V-v-very important," agreed Blink, blinking up at the Brigadier from his position on the hall floor.

Brigadier Fox's gaze flitted from one speaker to the next as the four friends awkwardly introduced themselves. His face was grim.

"I don't know," he said, finally. "Here I am, minding my own business, just about to go for a quiet evening stroll, when all of a sudden I find my door blocked by otters, rabbits, crows and...er..." He peered at Hammy. "and...things."

Old Crow flapped his wings in an attempt to show some confidence.

"We're sorry, sir, if we startled you. But we did knock. Apparently you did not hear us and we were just about to knock again when you...er...opened the door and gave us a bit of a start.

"But we are here on very important business to ask your help in a matter of great urgency."

The Brigadier frowned. "Humph! What sort of business can it be that concerns me if it concerns otters, rabbits, crows and...er... things?" He again looked curiously at Hammy.

Jumbles Wood

Now Hammy was normally a pretty quiet fellow. He was unused to the ways of Jumbles Wood and he had never seen a fox before. He was not normally given to losing his temper, but he was just about getting fed up with the way folk were talking about him since his escape from the Humans.

Nearly everyone he had met had commented about his name and the fact that he had no tail and he could stand no more. Now this strange looking creature dressed in an absurd red uniform had twice called him a "thing."

Hammy stepped forward and stared angrily up at the Brigadier. "I'm not a 'thing', I am a guinea pig," he said. "What's more, I'm proud of being a guinea pig and, before you say anything else, I proud that I haven't got a tail because I think tails are stupid things to have hanging about behind you."

Old Crow winced. Snuff Rabbit gulped. Blink Otter tried to make himself disappear into the Brigadier's hall carpet. And Hammy, suddenly catching sight of the enormous bushy tail which sprouted from the Brigadier's scarlet trousers, felt his courage drain away.

"Oh…I'm sorry," he said in a very small voice.

Brigadier Fox stared at the little guinea pig, surprised, for a few moments. Then he laughed loudly.

"Well said, little 'un," he barked. "That's what I like to hear. Plenty of spirit. You are quite right – I shouldn't have called you a 'thing'. Very uncivil of me."

The four friends were speechless. This was not the sort of reaction they had expected from the infamous fox.

Brigadier Fox looked from one to another, his gaze finally resting on Old Crow.

"Don't I know you? Old Crow, isn't it? Darned if I know why they called you old, mind you. I can remember you being born."

Old Crow preened himself. "I am now considered…ahmm…one of the senior citizens of Jumbles Wood. As a jackdaw I am…errm…considered chief among the crows."

"Ha! Who by?" laughed the fox. "Not by anyone of any account, I'm sure. Why, there's only a handful of the REALLY senior citizens left these days. You youngsters don't know what you are talking about.

"I can remember the good old days, when life was tough in Jumbles Wood. It was a case of the survival of the fittest. You have it easy these days – you don't know what it is to have to struggle.

"Why, in the days of the Great War...."

Just how long the old fox would have chattered on is not certain. But Hammy felt enough time had already been wasted.

"It's on a matter of war that we have come to see you," he said, firmly.

Brigadier Fox stopped and stared at his visitors one by one.

"War! What about war? We're not going to have another war, are we?" His eyes flashed and his whiskers twitched.

"I'm afraid we are," said Snuff. "In fact, Jumbles Wood seems likely to be invaded."

The Brigadier's whole attitude immediately changed. He looked swiftly left and right and then into the dark woodland behind the four friends.

"Say no more," he rapped. "You don't know who may be listening. Come into the house, all of you."

He ushered the four animals in through the big door and closed it firmly behind them, slamming home two big bolts and turning a huge brass key in the lock.

"Come into my study. We won't be overheard there."

CHAPTER 6

In the fox's lair

Brigadier Fox led the way down a dark, thickly carpeted hall and flung open a solid wooden door. They filed into a large room, with wood panelled walls, a large fireplace with a huge mantelpiece over it, laden with cups, trophies and polished brass shell cases.

The brigadier seated himself behind an enormous desk that was even bigger, older and more elaborately carved than the one at Snuff's Oak. Then he motioned to the others to be seated in four large, leather padded armchairs.

Snuff and Hammy had a bit of trouble climbing into the chairs and felt somewhat lost when they finally made it. Old Crow perched on the back of another chair. Only Blink Otter really looked comfortable in his chair – and even his feet failed to reach the floor.

"Now then," said the Brigadier. "What's all this about wars and invasion?"

Old Crow, Snuff Rabbit and Hammy all began to speak at once. Then they all stopped. Then they all started again.

"One at a time," barked the Brigadier. "You!" He pointed at Hammy. "You seem an alert fellow. You start."

Hammy began, nervously at first, but soon warming to his story. He told of his escape from the Human's house, his journey and his arrival in Jumbles Wood. Snuff then took over, explaining how Blink Otter had carried the word through the land as he delivered the milk.

Then Old Crow told of his flight over the Human house, the meeting of all the animals at Snuff's Oak and how it had been decided to ask the Brigadier for help.

He DID manage to give the impression it had been his own idea to visit the fox, but apart from that he managed to tell the tale without too much boasting or blustering.

Finally, Snuff said: "We thought, sir, that as we were faced with a war situation, we needed somebody with military experience."

Brigadier Fox nodded briskly. "Quite right too. If Humans are involved we shall need every bit of military experience we can muster."

He paused, drummed his paws on the desk and gazed up at the ceiling, muttering quietly under his breath.

The four friends sat motionless, all watching the Brigadier. They knew he was thinking deeply and dared not speak for fear of interrupting his train of thought.

Finally the fox said briskly: "We must mobilise at once."

"Mobilise?" said Blink. "What do you mean?"

"I mean…we must raise an army. Start training. Send out scouts. Appoint officers…that will be difficult with so few experienced fellows about.'"

"Are there ANY other experienced military men about?" asked Old Crow.

"I doubt it. It's a long time since the Great War. I was only a young fella myself then."

He folded his arms and thought some more.

"Is Old Badger still getting about much?" he asked.

Snuff nodded. "He is – he came to the emergency meeting and spoke. But he doesn't seem to be very interested in doing anything. He says he is too old."

"Too old be blowed!" retorted the Brigadier. "If he's too old, then so am I – and I am CERTAINLY not too old when my country needs me.

"Old Badger always was a bit lazy. Always did need somebody to tell him what to do. That's why he never got any rank, y'know."

"W-what's rank?" asked Blink.

Brigadier Fox pointed to the brightly coloured ribbons on his uniform.

"That is. I won my rank in battle too. It gives you authority. Power. You need somebody with plenty of rank to command an army."

"You seem to have plenty of rank, sir," said Hammy, gazing with admiration at the coloured ribbons.

"Quite right, young fella. You certainly came to the right place for advice on military matters.

"But I shall need some help. G.O.C must have a brigade commander, platoon commanders, etc. Yes, I will need help…"

His voice faded away into a muttering and a murmuring, punctuated by a drumming of his paws on his desk..

"Old Badger might do – he seems pretty wise," ventured Hammy.

"Yes. He needs a bit of pushing, but he's useful with his hands. He could take charge of the engineers. I'll have a chat with him."

He broke off and looked at Hammy intently.

"You're a bright young fellow and you've lived with Humans. How do you fancy taking charge of Intelligence?"

Hammy gulped. Intelligence! He'd never thought he had too much of that.

"What do you mean?" he asked nervously.

"Intelligence – that's spying. Finding out what the enemy is doing. Going behind the enemy lines and so on. Very important work – and very dangerous!"

Hammy felt a thrill of excitement run down his furry back. Danger! Spying!

"I'll do my best, if you think I am suited," he said.

"Good – that's settled then – I'll give you the rank of captain."

Old Crow coughed.

"I've flown over the Human house and seen behind their…er…lines," he said.

Old Crow had been growing increasingly impatient as he had listened to the general conversation and heard the Brigadier handing out rank to badgers and guinea pigs. He would have thought that he, Old Crow, would have been an automatic choice for command. Yet two important posts had been filled and he had been overlooked.

"Air reconnaissance is useful, but it is always of secondary importance to intelligence gained on the ground," Brigadier Fox said, brusquely.

He turned to Blink Otter. "We'll need somebody to take charge of naval forces. How do you fancy the rank of Admiral?"

Blink blinked. He hadn't really expected to be in the running when rank was handed out, so to be offered the job of an Admiral was indeed a pleasant surprise. In his mind's eye, he pictured a little brass plate like the Brigadier's, outside his dairy and bearing the inscription: "Blink Otter. Admiral of the Fleet."

Old Crow flapped his wings. "I live on Crow's Nest Hill," he remarked, testily. "And every ship has a crow's nest."

Brigadier Fox was not listening, however. He was looking at Snuff Rabbit.

"I shall need a personal assistant who will act as Liaison Officer between G.O.C. and the various armed forces. You seem a likely fellow for the job. The post will carry considerable rank – say, Major – as it will be necessary for you to communicate orders from the top to various commanders in the field."

Snuff hesitated. The idea of being a Major was quite appealing, but the notion of being the Brigadier's personal assistant was less attractive. He had not forgotten that the fox was reputed to have a liking for rabbit pie.

However, the Brigadier seemed to be concerned only with the crisis facing Jumbles Wood, so Snuff decided it was a post he could safely accept.

Old Crow sat in sullen silence as the rabbit voiced his thanks. He thought of mentioning that a personal assistant who could fly would be useful for carrying urgent messages quickly, but felt he had already humiliated himself enough. So he said nothing.

Brigadier Fox suddenly turned to him, however, and said: "There just remains the question of the Air Force."

The change that came over Old Crow was remarkable. The sullen look vanished from his face, his eyes resumed their usual brightness and his wings flapped importantly.

"I feel more than capable of taking charge of such an important force," he cackled.

Brigadier Fox rubbed his chin thoughtfully before answering.

"I have never been fully convinced of the value of air power," he said.

"Although in this particular case the enemy do possess flying machines of immense size and power, they cannot operate close to the ground and certainly cannot penetrate beneath the trees of our homeland.

"This being so, our Air Force is unlikely to have to undertake any aerial combat. Its role seems likely to be confined to reconnaissance and the support of ground troops.

"Whether such a force is of sufficient importance to justify an Air Commodore is doubtful…" he began.

But before he could say more, Old Crow broke in with a high pitched croak.

"I'm sure if I was made an Air Commodore I would make the Air Force play a more useful part in the war."

"Very well then," sighed the Brigadier. "I shall expect maximum support from all sections.

"Of course, I shall direct the war effort personally as Supreme Commander. My first task must be to establish a GHQ."

"What's that?" asked Blink Otter, forgetting for a moment that Admirals should not really ask such simple questions."

"General Headquarters, of course" rapped the Brigadier. "I would have the GHQ here, where all my maps and things are, but unfortunately it will be too far from the battlefront. I need somewhere in a central position."

"You would be very welcome to use my house," said Snuff quickly, anxious to impress in his new role of personal assistant to the Brigadier.

Even so, he was somewhat taken aback when the fox replied: "An excellent suggestion, Major. Snuff's Oak is, as I recall, ideally located.

Snuff was not only surprised by such ready acceptance of his suggestion, but also by being addressed as "Major".

"Er, very good, er…sir," he replied.

The Brigadier then turned to each of his new commanders.

"Captain Hammy – you can make an instant start. Enrol more secret agents and infiltrate the enemy positions. I suggest a Mole Patrol for maximum security.

"We must know the Human intentions as soon as possible so we can deploy our troops. Report to me as soon as you can."

Hammy stood up and saluted. He wasn't quite sure how he knew, but somehow he did know that soldiers, even Secret Agents, saluted senior officers.

"Right away, sir," he said, wondering how he was going to form a Mole Patrol when he didn't even know any moles.

But the Brigadier had already passed on to Blink Otter.

"Admiral, start an immediate and urgent survey of all available river craft and find out how they can be adapted for military use. Also investigate how a water-borne attack can be mounted on enemy territory."

Blink prefaced his salute by a violent attack of blinking, but eventually managed to indicate his acceptance of the instructions.

Brigadier Fox was already speaking to Old Crow.

"You can start effective operations quicker than any of us," he said. "Form squadrons of varying types from among the birds of the woods.

"Also start immediate and continuous aerial observation of enemy territory, particularly the stronghold at the house. Liaise with Secret Agent Guinea Pig at all times."

Old Crow preened himself and cackled: "Yes sir, right away sir," in what he hoped sounded an efficient military manner.

Brigadier Fox turned to Snuff.

"Major, you and I shall now commence moving GHQ to Snuff's Oak."

He glanced at the clock on the mantelpiece.

"We'll meet there at this time tomorrow."

The four friends bade the Brigadier goodnight and hurried back home. The winding, overgrown path was even darker now and very little moonlight filtered through the lattice work of branches overhead. But somehow the journey did not seem half as scary as previously.

All four of them felt they had done the right thing in going to see the Brigadier. The problem of the Human invasion was now in capable hands.

CHAPTER 7

The mole patrol

Secret Agent Hammy did not have any trouble forming a Mole Patrol. Snuff knew a family of moles who lived quite near his home so it took only a few minutes the following morning to enlist four strong, healthy moles into the new Jumbles Wood Army.

Conscious of the fact that Brigadier Fox wanted early intelligence of enemy activity, Hammy set off at once with the four moles, heading for the Human house. The party was unarmed and carried no equipment other than five spades.

Hammy's plan was to get as close as possible to the Human stronghold and then dig a tunnel under the fence which, he remembered, surrounded the garden. The four moles were, of course, expert tunnellers and Hammy himself was quite experienced in underground work.

He had only a rough idea of what life in a Human stronghold was like. He had to admit he had no memories of preparations for war on the part of the "enemy". Indeed, his recollections of the small boy and girl who had fed him in his cage were that, in their own way, they were doing their best to be kind to him.

Still, wiser folk than he in Jumbles Wood, regarded the Human presence as a serious threat so it was clear that war was likely. After all, his only experience of life before the Human house was at the pet shop, so he had to admit he was hardly qualified to judge.

Fortunately, bushes and other undergrowth provided good cover for the Mole Patrol to within a few yards of the Human's fence. This meant that only a short tunnel was necessary and four moles, assisted by an enthusiastic guinea pig, made short work of the task.

There was a minor problem because moles were not accustomed to digging tunnels big enough for guinea pigs, but this was soon solved. In no time at all, the tunnel was complete, except for the entrance into enemy territory.

On Hammy's instructions, the moles had dug up through the roots of a small bush so that the entrance would be less likely to be discovered. Even so, the new secret agent took elaborate precautions before the final break through to the surface was made. One mole was sent back to the edge of the wood so that a message could be taken back to headquarters in the event of the mission being overtaken by disaster.

Two moles were left to guard the outside entrance to the tunnel with orders to shout a warning if danger threatened.

The oldest mole, who Hammy had made a corporal, was to guard the inside end of the tunnel, remaining below the surface.

Hammy himself decided to undertake the dangerous task of entering the enemy stronghold. He felt that as the officer in charge, this was his duty. A captain in the Jumbles Wood Army should never shirk his duty, he felt.

Inch by inch, Hammy raised his head out of the freshly dug tunnel. Below him, his back legs were firmly placed on the shoulders of the unprotesting Corporal Mole. As the corporal straightened his back, so Hammy's head emerged further from the hole in the bush.

Finally, however, the mole had risen to his full height, which was not very high, and Hammy could still see nothing of the enemy stronghold other than a tangle of branches.

"Higher!" he whispered.

"What was that?" enquired the mole, who was not hearing as well as he might have done without a guinea pig's foot in his ear. "I said HIGHER" hissed Hammy, as loudly as he dared.

The mole got the message and, grasping Hammy's ankles firmly in each paw, thrust him upwards.

Now, the mouth of the tunnel had not been dug with Hammy's little round stomach in mind. The moles had forgotten, when digging the final stretch, that it would not be a mole using it. So for a moment, Hammy stuck fast, half out of the tunnel.

"Ooooph!" he grunted.

Corporal Mole, below, taking this sound to be an order from his superior officer to push harder, did just that and Hammy was ejected from the narrow tunnel like a cork from a bottle. His arrival in the middle of the bush was, therefore, accompanied by a strangled "Urrrgh!" and a crackle of twigs he would have liked to have avoided.

For a moment, he lay perfectly still, his little ears straining for any sound that might indicate he had been heard.

"Are you all right?" It was the voice of the mole in the tunnel.

"Ssssshhh!" hissed the guinea pig, conscious that if noises continued like this he would not be a SECRET agent much longer.

Jumbles Wood

No further sound came from the tunnel and all seemed quiet beyond the shelter of the bush, so Hammy crawled forward on his stomach, an inch at a time, until he could peep out between the leaves.

What he saw sent a chill down his spine. Only a short distance across the open garden were row upon row of soldiers!

As has already been stated, Hammy had not had a wide experience of life in the world beyond the pet shop. Never, until the previous night, when he had met Brigadier Fox, had he ever seen a soldier.

But now, as he stared with alarm from the shelter of the bush, he had no difficulty in recognising the Humans arrayed before him. They all wore scarlet uniforms, similar to that worn by the brigadier. They all carried swords. And they were all standing rigidly at attention.

A number of warlike machines stood around them and, even as he watched, a small wheeled vehicle carrying several more soldiers, shot into view from behind a low wall constructed of sand. The vehicle came to a halt in front of the assembled soldiers.

At the same instant, Hammy became aware of another Human – the boy who had sometimes fed him when he was a prisoner – striding towards him with a large brown dog at his side. Even as he watched the dog sniffed and rushed, barking, towards the bush.

Hammy waited to see no more. With a squeak of alarm he dived headlong into the tunnel, showering bits of earth and small stones on to the startled mole below.

Behind him he was vaguely aware of considerable noise and confusion. The barking of the dog, the boy shouting and the pounding of feet on the ground.

For a moment, Hammy thought he was safe, but in his frantic dash he had forgotten the difficulty he had encountered in getting out of the tunnel. The well rounded tummy that had wedged itself so obstinately on the outward journey, was no more inclined to go through the hole on the way back.

Hammy again found himself stuck, this time with his head, shoulders, chest and arms inside the tunnel while his furry rear end, and wildly kicking legs, remained above ground. There he hung, upside down, puffing and blowing with excitement, while Corporal Mole gazed up at him in amazement.

"Quick!" he gasped. "Pull me down."

The mole was not very tall, a fact which had contributed to Hammy's problems when he got stuck going up through the hole. Now the velvety creature's lack of stature was again a cause for anxiety.

For even when standing on tip toe, he could not reach the flailing paws above him.

Gritting his teeth, the mole jumped, grabbed at a paw – and missed.

Hammy puffed and grunted and expected at any moment to feel the dog's teeth on his back legs. The mole jumped again – and missed again.

"Keep still," he hissed. Hammy did his best and the mole jumped again.

This time paws met and clasped each other firmly in midair. For a moment, the combined weight of guinea pig and mole was insufficient to dislodged the furry stomach from the hole.

Then Hammy took a deep breath, pulled in his tum as much as he could – and fell, amid a shower of earth and stones.

"Oooph!" exclaimed Corporal Mole, as all the wind was knocked out of his small, velvety body by the furry avalanche.

The two animals rolled in a tangle on the floor to gaze in horror at flashing white teeth and glaring eyes in the hole in the tunnel roof above them. Secret Agent Captain Hammy had been released not a moment too soon.

Above them, the dog snarled, frustrated at seeing his quarry so close and yet beyond his reach. For if the guinea pig had been barely small enough to fit through the opening, the dog was far too big.

"Phew!" gasped Hammy. "That was close. Thanks, Corporal.

The mole was still not happy.

"Can the brute get through?" he asked anxiously.

Hammy looked up.

"No – not without quite a bit of digging. But we'd better clear off because he might start doing just that."

As if he had only just then thought of the idea, the dog began to scrabble at the edge of the hole with his front paws, showering the two animals with rubble.

They fled, pausing only to warn the other two moles on guard at the other end of the tunnel and the one at the edge of the wood. The five of them didn't stop running until they were back at Snuff's Oak.

CHAPTER 8

The hero's report

In the clearing by Snuff's Oak, Major Snuff Rabbit, a baton under his arm, was drilling a platoon of young foxes, all dressed in khaki battledress. They marched smartly up and down the clearing with great precision.

Old Crow was perched in a nearby tree, lecturing an assembly of birds on the finer arts of aerial warfare, occasionally referring to a large book on the subject which had been loaned to him by Brigadier Fox.

The Brigadier himself, now also wearing khaki, with a smart green beret, was standing by a table covered with maps, occasionally waving his arms and talking earnestly to Old Badger.

Old Badger was also dressed in khaki, although his appearance was not quite so strictly military as that of the fox. It was hard for the casual onlooker to guess exactly why he didn't look more soldier-like, but it was probably due to a certain lack of enthusiasm for the job in hand.

After all, Old Badger, despite being given the rank of Colonel, had been pressed into service rather unwillingly.

Hammy dismissed the Mole Patrol after promoting Corporal Mole to sergeant in gratitude for his efforts. Then he marched briskly up to the brigadier, saluted smartly and said: "Captain Hammy reporting – Sir!"

It really was a fine, military performance and Hammy felt rather proud of it. He also felt something of a hero after his narrow escape in the Human stronghold.

Brigadier Fox returned his salute briskly. After receiving a glare from the brigadier, Old Badger saluted too, although rather in a manner which suggested he thought the whole affair was rather foolish.

"You may make your report in front of Colonel Badger," said Brigadier Fox. "We are in urgent need of intelligence."

The newly appointed colonel silently wished that his superior officer would speak for himself, but said nothing.

"It was terrible" began Hammy. "I have never been so frightened…" But before he could say more, Brigadier Fox interrupted.

"Reports must be kept short and factual. I will decide what is terrible or frightening. You just tell us what happened."

Hammy felt a little deprived. Somehow, he felt that if the brigadier had been through what he had just been through, he would have given a very colourful report. However, orders were orders, so he told the story of the mission quickly and without any frills.

Brigadier Fox listened intently, his tail occasionally swishing back and to. Finally, he slapped his paw down on the map table and exclaimed: "Terrible! Frightening!"

Hammy resisted the temptation to say "I told you so." He had already learned enough about military life to realise that rank gave certain privileges, one of which was the sole right to use the most dramatic words.

His mission was not terrible, exciting or dangerous until or unless the brigadier said so. However, the brigadier HAD said so, now, so Hammy once again felt something of a hero.

Even Colonel Badger's interest was stirred sufficiently by the story for him to ask, mildly: "What does it all mean?"

"Trouble – that's what it means," declared Brigadier Fox.

He turned and called across the clearing. "Major Snuff! Air Commodore Crow! Staff conference immediately!"

Old Crow was there in a flash, his wings a blur of high speed motion. Snuff, who still hadn't got used to the idea of being a major, required several calls.

"Sorry," he puffed when he finally ran over. "I didn't realise you were speaking to me."

"Some people are just not suited to rank," remarked Old Crow, spitefully. He felt he could combine the Roles of Air Commodore and Personal Assistant to the brigadier quite adequately. Being the sort of person he was, he also felt quite competent to be Admiral of the Fleet, Secret Agent and, perhaps, even Supreme Commander as well. But this was just Old Crow. He couldn't help himself and everybody knew it.

"Where is the Admiral?" demanded Brigadier Fox.

For a moment, nobody connected the grand title with the somewhat nervous otter who delivered their milk each morning. Then Snuff Rabbit, whose job it was to KNOW where all the others were, said: "He's surveying river craft, sir."

"Well – we can't wait for him. We have important intelligence of the enemy's intentions and we must take quick action before they can attack."

Hammy was startled. "Is an attack on the way then?" he asked.

Jumbles Wood

He knew he had seen alarming sights in the Human stronghold, but nothing to indicate that the Humans were preparing to invade Jumbles Wood soon. Even the attack by the dog would not have happened if he, Hammy, had not gone spying in the Human's territory.

But, he decided, Brigadier Fox must be applying his military mind to the situation as reported by his intelligence service. With his experience he saw the possibility of imminent attack.

The brigadier began. "The old Jumbles Wood Army fought two wars," he said. "One was the Great War, of which some of you may have heard. That was a war between ourselves and the animals of Green Valley…"

"Where's Green Valley?" asked Hammy.

"Green Valley does not exist any more. But it used to be north of here. Human's moved in and built their huge houses there. The animals were forced to leave and came here.

"Their leaders were, er, unpleasant fellows who thought they should have the best places in Jumbles Wood for themselves.

"We thought differently, however, and the war broke out with the Jumbles Wood Army fighting to protect Jumbles Wood. We won, of course, and the Green Valley animals had to look for homes elsewhere, although a few of them did settle in with us and became Jumbles Woodlanders."

He coughed and shrugged his shoulders. "We were most gracious in our hour of triumph."

Snuff asked: "What about the first war?"

"Before my time," said the Brigadier. "I've heard it involved Humans, horses and packs of dogs hunting foxes and otters. Don't know how it ended but I'm still here and so are the otters.

"But all that is history. We have our own war to worry about now - and we need to act swiftly. One thing I remember from the Great War was that we spent a lot of time trying to persuade the Green Valley animals to go somewhere else.

"But while we were talking, they were preparing in secret, to attack us. Then when they did attack, we withdrew from part of Jumbles Wood hoping that they would be content to stay there and leave the rest to us.

"However, they simply saw this as a sign of weakness and tried to push us out of Jumbles Wood altogether. It was then that we fought back and, thanks to some brilliant leadership, managed to drive them back.

"This taught me a valuable lesson. When threatened, it is better to stand up for yourself from the very start. Then you will taken seriously. If we can show the Humans we mean business, they may go away – or at least not come any nearer."

Old Crow raised a wing.

"From what I can see, it looks as though the Humans plan to build more houses – each one nearer to Jumbles Wood," he said.

"Then the quicker we act the better," replied the Brigadier. "I want reports from all commanders in the field on how each one would suggest we mount our attack. We do have one advantage – the element of surprise. The Humans will not be expecting us to attack them."

It was agreed that each of the commanders would prepare plans overnight and return for a conference of war the next day.

Brigadier Fox told them: "I have my own ideas, of course, but I would like to see what my commanders in the field think before I announce my masterplan."

CHAPTER 9

The war conference

The next morning, Snuff Rabbit, Hammy, Blink Otter and Old Crow all presented themselves to Brigadier Fox in the room at Snuff's Oak that he had converted into his headquarters.

Each was laden with papers and maps – and each was bleary-eyed after being awake most of the night

Brigadier Fox, equally bleary-eyed, was in conference with Colonel Badger when they arrived – although as usual, the old badger seemed most unconcerned by the crisis facing Jumbles Wood. He was the only one present who appeared to have slept well. While the brigadier paced up and down the room, waving his arms, talking excitedly and occasionally pausing to thump his desktop with his paw, Colonel Badger simply sat, nodding occasionally.

The four friends waited patiently while the brigadier blustered on about supplies, lines of communication, intelligence, weather forecasts and the like. Eventually, they knew, the brigadier would calm down and allow them to present their reports. But they also knew it was better to be patient than to try and interrupt the fiery old fox.

At last, the Brigadier stopped pacing and stared at each of them in turn, almost as if he had only become aware of them.

"Well – what have you to tell me? Something useful I hope – or are you all stupid like this old fool of a badger?"

Colonel Badger nodded agreement before suddenly realising what had been said.

"Here, I say, old fellow…" he began. But then stopped in mid-sentence as the brigadier turned a withering look in his direction.

"Have you all prepared reports?" the Brigadier went on, now totally ignoring the uncomfortable badger.

The four friends nodded.

"Well then, out with it! Who's going first?"

Old Crow coughed, flapped his wings and spoke. "I have thought long and hard…"

Jumbles Wood

Brigadier Fox sighed and, under his breath, said: "Well that makes a change," but the recently appointed Air Commodore appeared not to notice the interruption. He went on: "...and I have come to the conclusion that the best and most decisive action we can take is a quick air-strike.

"I believe several squadrons of birds – the largest at my disposal – should dive-bomb the soldiers in the Human's headquarters. We will catch them off their guard...and the sooner we go the better."

Brigadier Fox scribbled on a pad in front of him and then looked at Blink Otter, who blinked furiously before spreading a map on the table.

"We have discovered that a stream, which flows into Deep River, passes close to the Human house and even closer to the land where they appear to be going to build more houses. We propose that, by night, teams of otters and voles should block the stream with stones, causing the stream to burst its banks and flood and whole area. That should make them think twice about building more houses."

The Brigadier scribbled furiously on his pad and then turned to the guinea pig.

Hammy coughed nervously.

"My plan involves a large group of moles burrowing under the fence around the Human house, emerging the other side and charging at the soldiers. The operation would be carried out at night when we would not be seen - and when the Human's dog would be locked up in his kennel. I believe we could be in and out before the soldiers knew what had hit them."

Brigadier Fox made more furious notes and then turn to glower at Snuff.

"And what stroke of military genius have you come up with?" he demanded.

Snuff hesitated, shuffled his feet on the ground, coughed and hesitated again.

"Well...er...I thought...that is..." he began.

"Come on, come on," snapped the fox. "You can't have come up with anything much more hare-brained than the others."

Old Crow, Blink Otter and Hammy looked at each in dismay. It appeared the brigadier didn't think much of any of their plans.

"Well," said Snuff, again, "Actually I had thought of something very similar to Hammy's plan, except that I had rabbits burrowing under the fence instead of moles. The tunnels would be bigger, allowing larger animals to get through..."

He broke off as the brigadier dropped his pen noisily on the map table.

There was a brief silence and then the brigadier leapt to his feet.

"Rubbish!" he barked. "Absolute rubbish! I have never heard anything so ridiculous. It's a good job I have a few ideas of my own. I have listened to all your plans, which apparently have taken you all night to prepare. I have been very patient.

"But I have come up with my own strategy, which came to me in a flash."

Colonel Badger broke the silence which followed.

"What exactly do you propose...er...sir?" he asked.

Brigadier Fox sat down at the table again.

"It is obvious," he said. "What we need is a simultaneous attack by air and land, supported by diversionary tactics involving the flooding of the nearby land. We would have birds – the largest available to us – dive-bombing the soldiers in the garden while, at the same time, rabbits and moles penetrated the enemy defences through tunnels dug beneath the fence.

"While all this is going on, otters and voles would construct a dam on the stream leading to Deep River, causing the stream to burst its banks and flood the land where the Humans are planning to build more houses.

"That should give them something to think about!"

"Brilliant!" exclaimed Old Crow, anxious to please. "A master stroke. Only a military genius could come up with a plan like that."

Colonel Badger rubbed his chin thoughtfully.

"Actually," he said, slowly, "It's the four plans drawn up by the four of you, all jumbled up into one."

"Jumbled up! What do you mean, jumbled up?" exclaimed Brigadier Fox.

"What I have done is join together the confused ramblings of four inexperienced officers and welded them together into a master plan – a strategy for ultimate victory!"

"It might work," said Hammy. "Each one of our plans would cause the Humans a bit of inconvenience, but all four of them together would give them a real shock."

Snuff said: "I particularly like the flood plan – Humans don't like water much, from what I have heard. They don't even like going out in the rain."

"It's agreed, then," said Brigadier Fox, briskly. "We will have to plan carefully. The timing will be very important. Training is essential if we are to get everything right – and we have no time to waste.

"Each of you must go away, recruit suitable animals for your part of the strategy and commence training immediately. In the meantime, we must post guards to keep watch on the Human house night and day so that if they do anything unexpected we are ready for it."

He folded up his maps and marched out of the room without so much as another word.

Jumbles Wood

CHAPTER 10

Preparing for war

So it was that the animals of Jumbles Wood started preparations for their attack on the Human house.

Day and night they worked. Old Crow gathered together as many large birds as he could find, including his fellow rooks from a nearby rookery, a pair of owls and a woodpecker.

Blink Otter commenced training his waterborne forces for their important task of building a dam across the stream. It was vital, he knew, that the dam was finished at just the right moment, if it was to make the stream burst its banks at the same time as the attack began on the Human house.

Snuff and Hammy recruited teams of rabbits and moles, issued spades and began the difficult task of deciding exactly where the tunnels should be constructed. Most of their work had to be done at night so that the Humans would not see what was going on.

All the time, Brigadier Fox, attended by a somewhat reluctant Colonel Badger, paced briskly about his headquarters in Snuff's Oak, drawing up plans, consulting maps and pouring through ancient books on military strategy.

Eventually he called another council of war and Snuff, Hammy, Blink and Old Crow gathered anxiously in his office.

Brigadier Fox sat behind his desk and fixed each of his commanders with a stern eye.

"I have finalised the plans," he said – but I now need to know if you are all ready. We cannot afford to delay our attack much longer as the Humans appear to be making preparations to start building more houses."

Snuff spoke up: "Hammy and I have surveyed the house and decided the best place for our tunnels. We have rabbits and moles trained and equipped to start digging as soon as you give the word."

Blink Otter was about to speak, but he wasted a few seconds blinking which gave Old Crow time to get in first. As an Air Commodore, he was rather annoyed that Snuff had managed to get in before him and was making sure he wasn't left at the back of the queue by a mere Admiral."The air force is ready to strike," he said. "Not only have my birds been training regularly but they have also been flying over the Human house every minute of every day to see what is going on. The Humans have not made a single move that we have not seen."

"And what have they been doing?" enquired Colonel Badger, stifling a yawn but glad of the opportunity of making a contribution to the conversation.

"Er…nothing," admitted Old Crow.

Brigadier Fox nodded his head wisely.

"They might APPEAR to be doing nothing, but they don't fool me," he said. "It is the oldest trick in the book. Lull your enemy into a sense of false security. Make him think you are asleep when in fact you are wide awake!"

"I've been doing that for years," said Colonel Badger, yawning again.

Brigadier Fox turned to Blink Otter. "And what of the Navy?"

Blink stuck out his chest importantly.

"We are ready. We have boats ready to sail up the stream to a place where we can easily block it with rocks and old tree trunks. There's an old tree that has fallen in the water already so we can easily build a dam at this point."

"Excellent," said Brigadier Fox. "Everything seems to be ready – so we'll strike tonight."

Everyone looked startled. Everyone except Colonel Badger, that is. He had been having trouble keeping awake for some time and had chosen this precise moment to nod off.

"Can we do it that quickly?" asked Snuff.

"We must. It is essential to catch the enemy off-guard," said Brigadier Fox. "The sooner we strike, the more likely we are to succeed."

He opened a drawer in the desk and produced six watches.

"I have synchronised these watches," he said.

"Synchronised? What does that mean?" asked Blink, blinking rapidly as he always did when something was puzzling him.

Jumbles Wood

Brigadier Fox sighed. "You silly otter. It means I have set all the watches at precisely the same time. I want us to all launch our attacks at exactly midnight and if we each wear one of these watches we will all know when it is time to strike."

He handed a watch each to Snuff, Hammy, Old Crow and Blink – and was about to hand one to the old badger when the dozing colonel let out a gentle snore.

"Perhaps we only need five watches," he groaned. "I think Colonel Badger had best stay behind and guard headquarters."

CHAPTER 11

The night attack

The attack started out exactly as planned – on the stroke of midnight.

There had, of course, been some advance work necessary. Blink Otter's naval force had set sail earlier to make sure his team of otters and voles was in place to start building the dam.

Snuff and Hammy were also busy directing operations as their platoons of rabbits and moles started digging the vital tunnels.

Old Crow flew high above the Human house keeping watch. He saw the man take his dog for a walk and then put him in his kennel, securing him with a chain. He saw the lights in the house going out one by one as first the children and later the adults went to bed. Eventually he was able to report that the house was silent and in darkness.

Brigadier Fox, who had taken up a position on the fringe of the Jumbles Wood, behind the house, remained cautious.

"It could be a trap" he said, after the self-important crow had made his report. "They could be lying in wait for us."

Old Crow, who was feeling rather pleased that he was the only one of the four field commanders able to keep in touch with the brigadier, shrugged his black shoulders.

"I don't think so," he said. "The dog is in his kennel as usual – and he is chained up as usual. He can bark his silly head off but he won't be able to do much else.

"The soldiers are lined up in their usual place – in fact they haven't moved since I have been observing them. My dive bombers will soon polish them off.

"If the Humans in the house hear anything it will take them some time to come out. They'll want to put their clothes on first – they are not like us, you know. Our ground troops should have done their job and be well away by then."

Brigadier Fox nodded. "Perhaps you are right, Air Commodore Crow," he said. "You are perhaps wiser than I have given you credit for."

He looked at his watch.

"It is time to begin.."

Jumbles Wood

At exactly the same moment, the last rocks were moved into place in the dam, the rabbits and moles broke through the last few inches of soil to emerge in the Human garden and the assembled flocks of birds swooped low over the house. It was a perfectly synchronised attack.

A clock on the mantelpiece in the house was striking midnight, so the Humans asleep in bed heard nothing.

The dog in the kennel, however, did.

Max was accustomed to hearing the noises of wild creatures outside the garden of a night and generally took no notice, provided they kept OUTSIDE the garden. This night, however, he had found it difficult to get off to sleep. He was aware of rather more bird activity than usual so was only dozing as the attack began.

The first wave of birds was led by the two owls. Old Crow would have liked to have been first himself, of course, but it was night and the owls were more used to night flying.

Each bird was carrying a pine cone or an acorn and each one had practiced hard to make sure they could drop them exactly where they wanted. But it was dark and although most of them fell among the lines of soldiers standing guard in the garden, some clattered on the roof of the kennel.

Max awoke with a start and leapt out of the door – forgetting that he was on a chain. He had bounded no more than a few paces before he was pulled up short, the chain pulling on his collar and turning his ferocious bark into little more than a whimper.

A second wave of birds swooped low overhead and Max found himself peppered with more pine cones and acorns. When one struck him on the end of his nose he was almost beside himself with fury.

While all this was going on, dozens of rabbits and moles, led by Hammy and Snuff, poured out of the freshly dug tunnels and ran headlong towards the soldiers.

Hammy found himself among the enemy. He struck out with both front paws and sent several soldiers, in their red uniforms, reeling. He was surprised that none of the enemy appeared to fight back but so much was going on he had little time to think.

Three big rabbits put their shoulders to a large, imposing looking military vehicle and pushed it on its side. A platoon of moles pounced on a brightly painted sentry box and sent it flying. Snuff Rabbit used his strong back legs to kick out at a cannon, mounted on wheels, and knocked it over, leaving it useless with its wheels spinning madly.

Jumbles Wood

Overhead came the sound of beating wings as another squadron of birds swooped in, showering the whole area with more pinecones. The woodpecker landed on a wooden fort and noisily did what woodpeckers do best.

Snuff looked around him. Everywhere the enemy was in disarray. Soldiers lay on their backs, tanks and guns had been overturned. The ground was littered with missiles dropped by the birds. He decided the time had come to withdraw. If they stayed, he felt, there was a strong possibility of them being hit by the next lot of pinecones or acorns to fall from the sky.

"Back to the tunnels," he shouted. "We've done our job."

Snuff and Hammy knew exactly how many rabbits and how many moles had charged out of the tunnels. Despite the confusion of battle, they kept calm and counted them all as they ran back and disappeared, one by one, into the holes.

Hammy felt a certain guilt over the chaos that had been caused in the garden. It was, after all, a place he knew well, having lived there and he was still not sure in his own mind that the Humans were as much a threat as the other animals seemed to think.

"Everyone has gone," he told Snuff. "You go next and I'll follow."

Snuff, however, felt he should be the last to leave. He was, after all, a Major and the senior officer present. It was his duty to make sure everyone had left the danger area.

"No – you go first. I will follow you," he said.

"I insist that you go first," said Hammy.

The pair were so busy arguing that they forgot all about their own safety. But they were about to get a reminder.

A sudden roar shattered the silence of the night – and they turned to see Max the dog glowering at them.

The last few minutes had not been a happy experience for Max. Usually, his nights were spent in blissful sleep in his warm kennel. Seldom, if ever, was he disturbed by anything

But first he had been rudely awakened by the clatter of falling missiles on the kennel roof, then he had been peppered with pinecones and acorns from head to toe and then he had stood helpless, chained to his kennel, watching a horde of rabbits and moles running amok in the garden.

Now he saw these two animals, one who seemed strangely familiar to him, standing arguing in front of him.

He stared at the smaller one – and suddenly realised who it was.

"I know you," he snarled. "You are that funny little creature with no tail who used to live here. You're the one who made Mandy cry when you ran away."

Max was Robin's dog. There was no doubt about that. But he knew that Amanda was Robin's sister and he loved her too. He had been very upset to see the girl cry so much when her pet disappeared. He couldn't see what all the fuss was about himself. After all, the silly little creature didn't even have a tail. But there was no accounting for taste

Now he saw the creature again, apparently involved in some desperate plan to cause chaos in the garden. For the second time, Max forgot he was attached to a length of chain - and leapt towards the guinea pig with such force that the chain snapped.

Fortunately for Snuff and Hammy, the big dog lost his balance and fell sprawling on the ground in front of them. The two friends stared at the snarling dog for a split second – and then fled.

Snuff, with his strong back legs, reached the nearest tunnel in one bound and disappeared down it in a flash. Hammy, with much shorter legs, could only run as fast as they would carry him.

Max was on his feet in a flash and raced in pursuit, the broken chain flying behind him. He saw the scampering animal in front of him – and leapt.

Hammy, somehow sensing a tremendous effort was called for, threw himself forward, headfirst into the tunnel. Behind him he heard the dog's giant jaws clash together in a last desperate attempt to catch him. In the next instant he was tumbling headlong down the tunnel to land in a heap on top of Snuff Rabbit.

The pair disentangled themselves and stared in horror at the dog's glaring eyes and gaping jaws jammed in the mouth of the tunnel above them.

"He can't get us" gasped a trembling Hammy, remembering his previous escape from the dog. "He's too big to get through the hole."

A breathless Snuff Rabbit, brushed himself down and laid a gentle paw on his friend's shoulder.

"You are right – but I'll tell you one thing. It's a good job you haven't got a tail. If you had, you would have lost it tonight."

Back at headquarters in Jumbles Wood, Brigadier Fox assembled his field commanders and received their reports.

He smiled with satisfaction as Old Crow described how wave after wave of birds had swooped over the garden, causing chaos with their well-aimed missiles. His chest swelled with pride as he heard of the bravery of the rabbits and moles who had charged the enemy soldiers and left them a broken force.

And he was more than happy to hear Blink Otter report on the success of the dam builders.

Water was already overflowing from the stream and pouring down a slope to the area where the Humans appeared to be building more houses.

"We will not know the full effect of your efforts until morning," the brigadier told the blinking admiral. "But by daylight, the whole area should be flooded."

Hammy raised a paw and the brigadier motioned him to speak.

"I am a bit puzzled that we didn't meet with more opposition," he said. "I know we were hoping to catch the enemy by surprise, but I would have expected them to fight back in some way. Apart from the dog – who, as an animal, should have been on our side really – nobody tried to stop us at all."

"Funny creatures, dogs," observed Brigadier Fox. "They always seem to be on the Human's side. Horses and cats are a bit the same. Never could understand it."

Old Crow preened himself and puffed up his feathers.

"Air power, in my opinion, proved decisive. My squadrons had the enemy on the run before our... er... infantry even started."

"Here, I say," protested Snuff. "I think the rabbits and moles did a magnificent job. They were the ones who were in most danger – particularly after some silly bird bombed the dog kennel!

"Hammy would probably have been caught if he had possessed a tail!"

"That's enough," rapped Brigadier Fox. "I don't want any arguments about who did best. You all did well. It was a good night's work and it seems to have caught the Humans on the hop. But we have only won a battle – we have not yet won the war.

"We will have to be very watchful now to see what the Humans do next. They may still want to build more houses closer to Jumbles Wood. In fact if they do what they did in Green Valley, they might even build houses IN Jumbles Wood. That would be the end for us."

CHAPTER 12

The morning after

Robin and Amanda were having breakfast before they realised Father had not gone to work.

He came in, washed his hands and dried them on the kitchen towel, earning a look of rebuke from Mother.

"Did you hear anything during the night?" he asked.

Mother was getting milk from the 'fridge.

"Yes – I heard Max barking his head off. I was going to go down but then he stopped so I didn't bother."

"You should have woken me – I would have gone down."

"Why? Has something happened? I just thought he'd been disturbed by some animal outside the garden."

Father frowned. "Well, something has certainly happened, but I'm not sure what."

Robin looked up from his cereals. "What do you mean, Dad? Have we had burglars?"

"I don't know what we've had. The garden looks as though there's been some sort of a riot going on. Max has been out of his kennel – somehow he's managed to snap his chain.

"He's been digging all over the flower beds by the fence. There's soil all over the place.

"And all your soldiers have been knocked over."

"What!" Robin was on his feet and at the window in a flash.

He saw his model army camp in ruins. Toy soldiers were scattered all over the place and tanks and lorries overturned.

"Who's done that?" he exclaimed. "I spent hours building that."

Amanda said: "I always told you not to leave your stupid soldiers outside all the time."

Her brother looked at her. "You've not done it, have you. You are always going on about them…"

"No. Don't be stupid. I've got better things to do than that. It's probably Max if he's been out of his kennel during the night."

Father said: "I know Mandy didn't do it because she was in bed before I took Max for his walk last night. Everything was OK when I came back."

"It was about midnight when I heard Max barking," said Mother. "But surely he wouldn't do that – he's never done anything like that before."

"But there's something else," said Father. "The garden is full of pine cones and acorns. Hundreds of them. All around your army camp, Robin, and all around the dog kennel. I just don't understand it."

Mother looked out of the window.

"It looks almost as if there had been a gale during the night, with all that stuff lying around."

"Yes – except that there are no pine trees or oaks nearby. In fact, the nearest trees are 200 yards away and it would take a heck of a wind to blow anything that far, even if they were the right sort of trees."

"So what do you think has happened, Dad?" asked Robin.

"I just don't know, son. I've never known anything like it. It's almost as though…." he broke off as the telephone started to ring.

Father went into the hall to answer the call and Robin and Amanda continued eating their breakfast while Mother clattered pots and pans around the kitchen.

A few minutes later, Father returned. "Well, it never rains but it pours," he said, pulling on a coat.

"What's happened now?" asked Mother, seeing the worried look on her husband's face.

"The building site is under water and all the fields are flooded."

"Flooded!" exclaimed Mother. "I didn't know it had rained…."

"It hasn't. There hasn't been any rain all week. But somehow or other, everywhere is flooded. It sounds as if we have been lucky there. The water almost reached our garden – I would probably have seen it over the fence if I hadn't been so busy looking at the chaos inside the garden.

"Joe, the site manager, seems to think that stream across the field has burst its banks. But I can't see why. It has never done it before – I checked all the records going back for hundreds of years before I bought the land.

"We've got real problems if we find the land we're building on is subject to flooding."

"What are you going to do?" enquired Amanda.

Jumbles Wood

"I'm going to inspect the damage and have a look at the stream. I've got to find out what caused the flooding and then try and find a way of making sure it doesn't happen again. People are not going to want to buy houses if they are likely to get flooded all the time."

Father pulled on Wellington boots and left while Robin went out into the garden to examine his wrecked fort.

Amanda looked out of the window.

"I don't think this is a very lucky house," she said. "We've had nothing but bad luck since we've lived here. First we lost Hammy, then we had the garden wrecked and now the fields are all flooded."

She felt her eyes going moist as tears began to form at the thought of her missing pet.

"Don't be silly, dear," said Mother. "There's no such thing as an unlucky house."

Robin came back in from the garden.

"Mandy's right – it's certainly isn't a very lucky house. I'll have to build my camp again. All my soldiers have been knocked over, some of my tanks and lorries broken and it looks as though someone has been trying to drill a hole in the fort.

"Dad said it would be lovely living in the country, but I never expected anything like this. What are we going to do?"

Mother sighed.

"Your father will fix things – he always does," she said.

"He hasn't been able to find Hammy," said Amanda, fighting back her tears.

It was a Saturday, so Robin and Amanda didn't have to go to school. Breakfast over, Robin went out to repair his fort. Amanda helped Mother sweep up all the debris in the garden and do some jobs about the house.

Several hours later, father returned.

"Panic over," he said, pulling off his boots. "We've found the cause of the problem. A tree had fallen in the stream and all sorts of logs, stones and old tin cans had piled up against it to form a dam. Quite remarkable really, you would never think it could happen.

"But it didn't take Joe and I long to shift them and I've hired a pump to clear the flood water from the field. Everywhere will be as dry as a bone by next week and there's not much chance of it happening again. Let's face it, if it hasn't happened in a hundred years it is not likely to happen again."

Jumbles Wood

Mother frowned.

"I'm not happy about it," she said. "I've always thought it was a pity we had to build more houses. When you said we were going to build our own house in the country, I always thought of us being on our own, without any other houses nearby. You didn't say you were going to build a whole village."

"Village? What are you talking about? I'm am only talking about building about 20 houses. That's hardly a village – anyway we already have a village down in Green Valley."

"Well the people at the farm down the road don't like it," said Mother. "They say you'll destroy the wood…you'll be spoiling the countryside.

"I've heard people talking in the Green Valley Post Office, as well. They think we are turning the village into a town."

Father laughed. "They won't be saying that when the people who live in the new houses go into their Post Office to buy their groceries and their newspapers. They'll thank us then. And the farm shop will be selling more milk and eggs. I tell you – we will be good for the area.

"And I won't be destroying the wood. I'll be leaving quite a bit of it – not to mention the trees I will leave in the gardens of the houses. People like trees in their gardens – that's the beauty of building there. They won't have to plant new trees and wait for them to grow.

"It's not much of a wood anyway. I'm told there's an old tramp living in there. If we get rid of him we'll be doing the villagers a favour."

"Well it won't be much good for us if you build your houses and nobody buys them because they are worried about flooding," said Mother.

"I agree – that's why we have to keep quiet about the flooding. It won't happen again so there is no need for anyone to know about it."

Amanda went up to her bedroom and looked out of the window. From there she could look over the fields and see Jumbles Wood beyond.

She didn't really understand what her Mother and Father were arguing about. But she did think the fields, the river and the woodland looked nice. It would be a shame, she thought, if her father's new houses spoiled it all.

"Oh, Dad, " she said to herself. "Why did you have to be a builder?"

CHAPTER 13

Volunteers wanted

A full day and a full night had passed since the attack on the Human house. It had been a busy day for Old Crow and his bird squadrons for they had been flying almost continuously over the house, the adjoining fields and the place where the Humans were preparing to build more houses. They had been keeping a close watch on the Human activities below.

Each bird returned from its flight and went directly to Crows Nest Hill where Old Crow sat, looking very important and satisfied with himself, making notes of everything each bird had seen. He had found himself a large desk which, he privately admitted to himself, was not quite as impressive as the one at Snuff's Oak, but which was pretty good all the same.

Hammy and his mole patrol had been more busy during the night. They had bravely returned to the scene of the battle – taking care not to be seen – to take a close-up view of what damage had been done.

Blink Otter had taken a small canoe – a larger vessel would have been more likely to be spotted by the enemy – and paddled his way up Deep River and then up the stream to the point where he and his team had built the dam.

Snuff Rabbit and the sleepy Colonel Badger had spent the day with Brigadier Fox. It seemed to them that their main task at the moment was to listen while their commanding officer paced endlessly up and down his small office, waving his arms about and making all sorts of plans for future action, depending on how successful the raid had been.

"IF…" he kept saying, "IF we have inflicted serious damage it may be a good idea to strike again quickly. But IF, on the other hand, the damage is not as serious as we might have hoped for, it may be a good idea to strike again quickly anyway.

"IF, however, the enemy appears to be preparing a counter-attack, we should perhaps be taking up defensive positions. And IF…"

Colonel Badger sighed.

"If, if, if…" he said. "Wouldn't it be better to wait until we know what damage we caused before we start making more plans?"

"Nonsense," barked the irritable fox. "We must be prepared for all eventualities. We cannot afford to waste a moment. We must have a plan for this and a plan for that and another plan in case it is neither this nor that."

Snuff found it all rather puzzling.

"Well," he said. "We KNOW we did quite a lot of damage. Everyone there reported successful operations…"

Brigadier Fox eyed him sharply. "In the heat of battle, even the most battle-hardened troops often get a false impression," he said. "It is only when you go back and study the situation carefully and calmly that you get the full picture. But IF…"

So it went on, with Brigadier Fox literally wearing out Snuff's carpets as he paced up and down the office.

Eventually all the patrols returned from their missions and the brigadier called yet another meeting.

"I want to de-brief you all," he announced.

Blink Otter blinked. "De-brief?" he queried. "What is a de-brief?"

Brigadier Fox groaned. "I mean, I want you to tell me what you have seen," he said slowly.

"Then why didn't you say that?" Blink persisted.

Snuff gave him a dig in the ribs. "Sshhhh! We are in the army now. You can't ask the CO questions."

"CO? What's a CO?"

"You silly otter…the Commanding Officer!"

Brigadier Fox glowered at the pair. "Have you two quite finished?" he barked. "Can we start the de-briefing?"

Old Crow flapped his wings importantly. "I am ready to be de-briefed…sir" he cackled.

The fox turned a sharp eye towards the preening bird. "I will decide who is de-briefed first," he snapped.

Everyone fell silent as the fox rose to his feet, marched up and down the office and then sat down at the desk again.

He glared at Old Crow. "Air Commodore Crow – kindly give your report."

Old Crow coughed, cleared his throat and puffed out his chest to make himself look as imposing as possible.

He said: "The Human forces were devastated by our aerial bombardment. They were left in total disarray but…they have put everything back as it was before."

There were gasps from the assembled animals.

"Everything?" asked Brigadier Fox, forgetting for a moment, to bark in his usual military manner.

"Everything," said Old Crow. "The soldiers are all back at their posts, the armoured vehicles have all been replaced in their original positions and even the fort has been rebuilt. The section damaged by our Woodpecker has been replaced. And all the pine cones and acorns which we dropped have been swept up and put in a dustbin. We saw the Humans sweeping them up with a large brush."

A stunned silence greeted the Air Commodore's report. No-one knew quite what to say. But eventually Brigadier Fox regained his composure and turned to Hammy.

"Captain Hammy...does your intelligence confirm the Air Commodore's report?"

Hammy sighed. "I'm afraid it does. What's more, all the tunnels we dug under the fence to get into the garden have been filled in at both ends. Quite a lot of work would be needed to use them again."

The Brigadier turned to Blink Otter.

"Have you any better news for us, Admiral?"

For a moment, Blink, who had still not got used to the idea of being an admiral, wondered who the fox was talking to. Then he saw every eye in the room looking at him.

"W-w-well, I, that is we...don't have any g-g-good news at all. The dam we built has been completely removed from the stream which is now flowing fully again. The flooding in the fields has gone – and the Humans have got some sort of noisy machine pumping all the water from the building site back into the stream. It is virtually dry already."

The silence got even quieter as each animal digested the grim news.

It was Colonel Badger who eventually blurted out what each animal was individually thinking.

"In other words, we have all wasted our time," he said.

He thought for a moment, scratched his head, yawned and added: "I always thought it was a waste of time."

Snuff Rabbit stood up.

"It was not a waste of time," he said. "It has shown us that the Humans can re-build their defences and repair any damage we cause. But it does not mean we just give up. There must be something else we can do."

Brigadier Fox nodded. "There has to be a solution. Never say die, that's what I say. We must change our tactics."

Colonel Badger yawned again. "I don't see what we can do," he said. "We attacked simultaneously on land, on water and in the air. We caught the enemy by surprise. But in a day and a night they have rebuilt everything as if we hadn't done a thing. What is the point of doing the same again."

He looked at Brigadier Fox. "I don't have a military mind like yours, old friend, but I don't think there is a military solution to the problem."

Brigadier Fox's whiskers bristled and his handsome tail swished. "Nonsense," he barked. "There is always a military solution. It's just a matter of finding it."

Hammy had not said anything for a little while. As a newcomer to Jumbles Wood he was still reluctant to make suggestions. After all, even though he was a secret agent, he was only a captain, which didn't sound quite so grand a title as an Air Commodore, an Admiral, a Colonel or even a Major. He wasn't even sure if it was his place to have an opinion in military matters.

But on the other hand, he had lived with the Humans – in the grounds of the very house they had attacked. And if it hadn't been for him, it was quite likely the woodlanders would still not even know of the threat to their homes and way of life.

He had listened to everything everyone else had said and it seemed to him they were getting nowhere. So he decided things could not much worse if he had his say.

"I think…" he began, and every head turned towards him. "I think we have got to think again. We have to be cunning and perhaps try something completely different. Perhaps something that is not…er…military."

Brigadier Fox's whiskers bristled again.

"Now then, young fella," he said. "I have a good deal of respect for you. That's why I put you in charge of Intelligence. And I am all in favour of being cunning – we foxes are famous for it. I am also in favour of trying something different. But if we are not to use our military might, how can we possible repel the invaders?"

Hammy began to feel a little more confident.

"Well, so far, our military might has not been enough," he said. "It has hardly bothered the Humans at all. We have to be bold and imaginative...and I think we need help."

"Help? Who is going to help us?" replied the Brigadier, sounding a little irritable.

Hammy took his courage in both paws. "At our first meeting – before we even came to see you, sir, someone suggested asking for help from the Green Wizard."

Brigadier Fox swallowed hard, tried to reply but failed to make a sound. No-one else said a word – and Hammy took advantage of the silence to carry on.

"I don't know anything about this Wizard," he said. "I don't know who he is, where he lives or why he might help us. But someone did mention his name."

Old Crow coughed nervously. "It was me...but...well... we were desperate!"

"We still are desperate," said Hammy. "In fact, we are more desperate, because our first plan has failed. We asked the brigadier here to help with his military skills...which have proved very valuable, I'm sure...but we still face the threat of invasion. Desperate situations call for desperate measures. It seems to me that if we ask the Wizard for help, the worst that can happen is that he will refuse."

Brigadier Fox regained his composure.

"You are a stranger to Jumbles Wood, young fella. You can't be expected to know our ways. This is the first I have heard of this idea. The Wizard might live in the woods, but he is a Human himself. We can hardly expect him to help us against other Humans. He's more likely to help them."

Snuff Rabbit broke in.

"I'm not so sure. The more I think about this idea, the more I begin to think Hammy could be right. The Wizard lives with us in the wood. He chooses to do that rather than live with other Humans. He never does anything to harm any animals – and he never goes into the Human towns or villages. I've even heard rumours that he can speak with animals.

"If Jumbles Wood were to be taken over by Humans, his way of life would be threatened just as much as ours."

"But he's a Human," exclaimed the Brigadier. "We foxes don't trust 'em, you know. They have a nasty habit of chasing foxes with packs of dogs."

Snuff smiled. "We rabbits didn't trust foxes, sir. They…er…have a reputation for enjoying rabbit pie. But you have got your headquarters here in my house now and we are both fighting on the same side."

There was a lengthy silence and then the Brigadier banged his paw on his desk.

"By jingo, you're right, Major Rabbit," he exclaimed. "In normal times, the idea of a rabbit inviting a fox into his home would be laughable. But these are not normal times. We could well have a lot in common with the Wizard.

"I don't believe we should stop our military operations, but there is no reason why we should not approach the Wizard as well. There's nothing to lose. The question is, who is going to go and see him?"

"Our commanding officer," piped up Old Crow.

Brigadier Fox shook his head. "Much as I would like to go, I obviously can't. If things went wrong, it could mean you would lose your leader. Then where would you be?"

Colonel Badger, who had been following the conversation with his usual disinterest, resisted the temptation to suggest that the commanding officer would not be missed. Instead, he roused himself to say: "We did appoint an Animal Council when it was decided to seek your help, Brigadier. They..er…volunteered, if I remember rightly… and they are all still available."

Snuff Rabbit, Hammy, Blink Otter and Old Crow looked at each other. Each of them could think of a dozen reasons for NOT volunteering to visit the Green Wizard. But none of them would be the first to admit to being afraid.

Brigadier Fox solved their problem for them.

"When there's a dangerous mission to be carried out, there's nothing like a volunteer. So I am ordering each of you to volunteer."

CHAPTER 15

Off to see the Wizard

It was generally agreed that the expedition to meet the Green Wizard should travel during the day. It was a lengthy journey, even further than the one to Brigadier Fox's house, and to an even more remote part of Jumbles Wood, so the four "volunteers" wanted to make sure they did not have to face the added dangers of a journey by night.

Old Crow, of course, made much of the fact that he could fly to the Wizard's cave in a matter of minutes and even more of the fact that he considered it his duty to stay with the others. He said nothing about the fact that if he DID fly on ahead he would be on his own when he got there.

The first part of the journey followed the course of Deep River and the other members of the Animal Council were quick to agree to Blink Otter's suggestion that they travel this part in his boat. This was a good deal quicker and a lot less tiring on the legs.

Snuff, Hammy and Old Crow lounged comfortably in the little boat while Blink happily and expertly guided the vessel along the swift flowing river.

It was not often that Blink Otter felt important, but he knew that when it came to watery matters, he was the expert and that the others looked up to him for guidance.

But the next stage of the journey involved a difficult descent into a deeply wooded valley where, even during the daylight hours, the rough path between the trees and bushes was dark and gloomy. Few animals visited this part of Jumbles Wood and even fewer lived there.

The four friends made good progress, however, guided by Old Crow who fluttered above the heads of the other three, warning them of fallen trees or outcrops of rock which made parts of the route almost impassable. As a result, the party was able to make a number of detours to avoid the more difficult parts of the path.

As they got closer and closer to the sheer cliff in which the Wizard had his cave, the four spoke in lower and lower tones, finally stopping talking at all. The only sound was the scrabble of three sets of small feet on the stony ground and the flapping of Old Crow's wings.

None of them had been this close to the Wizard's cave before, so the surroundings were as strange and unknown to Snuff, Blink and Old Crow as they were to Hammy, who of course had very limited experience of life in the outside world. A native of South America he might be, but his previous life in a pet shop and a Human garden had not prepared him for such adventures. His little feet quickly became sore and his heart began to beat faster.

Blink would have much preferred to have still been gliding along the river in his boat and Snuff was not used to such long journeys over such rough and rocky surfaces.

Even Old Crow, who usually found flight virtually effortless, began to tire as he hovered above the rest of the party.

Just how far it was to the cave, none of them knew, for it was hidden in a cliff face surrounded by dense, overhanging trees. The Wizard, when he had made his home there, had clearly not wanted to be disturbed.

Suddenly, Snuff, who was leading the party, stopped.

"Listen," he whispered. "What's that noise?"

They all strained their ears – and all heard the strange sound. It was like nothing they had heard before and certainly not a sound made by anything furry or feathered.

"It's a Human voice," hissed Hammy. "But it's not like any Human voice I've heard before."

Old Crow settled on the ground next to Snuff. "I think it's a Human singing," he said.

"If it is, he should leave it to the birds," observed Blink.

"Well, at least if he is singing he must be in a good mood," said Snuff.

The four pressed on, Old Crow hopping along with the others now. Suddenly, they emerged from the undergrowth into a small clearing with a looming cliff at the far end. And there, in front of the black cave mouth in the rock face, was a Human sitting in front of a log fire on which was a large, steaming cauldron. It was the Green Wizard.

As the four friends stared at him, the Wizard suddenly stopped singing, turned towards them, smiled and said: "Hello – have I got visitors?"

The four friends stood transfixed. For once, even Old Crow was struck dumb. They stared at the Wizard, who rose from the rock on which he had been sitting, and beamed with pleasure.

He was a tall man, even for a Human, with long, tangled, grey hair which fell over his shoulders and a long, grey beard. His trousers were held up with a length of rope and on his feet he wore open-toed sandals. His face was brown and weather-beaten. In his hand, he held a long-handled spoon with which he had been stirring the contents of the steaming cauldron.

"Well, don't just stand there," he said. "It's not often I have visitors. Come and join me by the fire and have something to eat. You must have travelled far."

Old Crow finally pulled himself together and hissed at the others: "Shouldn't he be wearing a pointed hat?"

The Wizard laughed. "Everyone thinks I should have a pointed hat, and so I have. But I don't wear it all the time you know."

Blink Otter stuttered: "He knows what we are saying…"

"Of course I know what you are saying," laughed the Wizard. "I have lived in the woods with you for many years. I wouldn't be much of a wizard if I hadn't learned to speak your language, would I?"

Snuff Rabbit stepped forward, hesitated for a moment and then said: "Er…Mr Wizard. We have been sent by the animals of Jumbles Wood to ask you for help."

"I know that," responded the Wizard. "One of the troubles of being a wizard is that very few people – animal or Human - ever come to see you except when they want help. I haven't had an animal visit me for years and it is a long time since I have seen any Humans either. So I know you are looking for help and I know what sort of help you are looking for."

"You do?" gasped Old Crow, desperately trying to regain his composure. He was, after all, an Air Commodore and chairman of the Animal Council, so he should be taking a leading part in the conversation.

"Yes, I do. But, please come and join me for a meal. I am a poor host to leave you all standing there when there are places by my warm fire."

Hammy moved forward cautiously. He had lived with Humans so was perhaps less overawed at being in the company of a Human, even one who was a wizard.

"Come on, Hammy," said the Wizard. "If you sit down the others will as well."

Hammy gaped. "You know my name!" he exclaimed.

"Yes, and I also know the… er… rather amusing story of how you got it. But come, sit down…"

Hammy sat on a small rock and was joined by Snuff and Blink, who was blinking even more rapidly than usual. Old Crow fluttered a few yards to settle on a larger rock, immediately opposite the rock on which the Wizard had been sitting. It was, he thought, more fitting for an Air Commodore and chairman of the Animal Council.

The Wizard produced four bowls and ladled steaming soup from the cauldron.

"Let us eat, before we discuss your problem," he said.

The four friends were a little hesitant at sampling the contents of the cauldron. They had heard tales of magic potions, poisons and other strange brews made by the Wizard. How did they know they would not be put to sleep, turned into statues or even transformed into some other sort of creature?

"Have no fear," smiled the Wizard. "This is just a good, nourishing vegetable soup which I made myself this morning. See, I shall try some myself."

He poured some of the soup into a fifth bowl, produced a large spoon and swallowed a large mouthful of the steaming concoction. "Delicious," he declared. "Even though I say so myself."

Hammy sipped at the soup and then tried a larger mouthful. "It IS rather good," he said.

The other three bent over their bowls and tasted the soup. All were hungry after their trek through the woodland and all agreed that the soup tasted good. Within minutes all four bowls were empty.

"Ah," said the Wizard. "It is good to see my cooking is appreciated. Please have some more."

This time there was no hesitancy. All four bowls were held out while the Wizard ladled more soup from the cauldron – and all four were swiftly emptied.

"That was very nice, sir," said Hammy, licking his whiskers. "We were all pretty hungry and I only hope we have not...er...left you short for yourself."

"No, not at all," laughed the Wizard. "I have plenty more in the pot and can easily make more if I run short. I also have a delicious crab-apple and blackcurrant pie which we can sample in a little while. But first, let us discuss your problem."

Old Crow puffed out his chest importantly. While he had been drinking his soup, he had been preparing what he considered to be an inspired speech to inform the Wizard of the dangers facing Green Wood.

"Well, sir," he began. "We are in a state of war...we are fighting to save Jumbles Wood from an invasion...an invasion that could leave every animal in the wood without a home..."

Jumbles Wood

"Yes, yes, I know all about that," said the Wizard. "There is not much that happens in or around Jumbles Wood that I don't know about.

"I know about the new Human House on the other side of the wood, and of the Human plans to build more houses and roads. I also know how you have formed an army, under the command of Brigadier Fox, and how you attacked the house and flooded the land nearby.

"It was an ingenious plan and all the animals and birds of Jumbles Wood showed great courage. You should be proud of yourselves for you did inflict considerable damage on your enemy. It was a magnificent effort, but..."

He paused for a second and Snuff finished the sentence for him: "...but we failed."

Blink Otter blinked furiously and added: "Despite everything we did, the Humans had repaired all the damage within a day."

Old Crow sighed and intoned: "It would seem that the Humans are able to resist the greatest force we are able to muster and simply carry on as if we were not even there.

"Brigadier Fox thinks we can fight on, but I don't think any of the rest of us thinks we have a chance."

The Wizard smiled. "The brigadier is a military man, with a military mind. This means he will always think of some other tactic, some other manoeuvre, some other operation. Military people are like that – and it is a good thing too, for there are times when it is important to fight for what you believe in.

"But in this case, I am afraid that no matter what your army does, the Humans will win in the end. They have the power, the machines and the strength."

"Does this mean you can't help us?" asked Hammy, gloomily.

"No, it does not," replied the Wizard. "You have come to me for help and I believe I can help you. But it will involve careful planning and a little magic. It may also, I fear, mean great sacrifice – and it will need a little help from the Humans themselves."

"Help from the Humans – why should they help us?" queried Old Crow.

"I am a Human and you have to come to me for help."

"Yes – but you live with us in Jumbles Wood. If all the trees are chopped down and more houses and roads are built, you will lose your home just as we lose ours. That is why we came to you...that, and because you are a Wizard."

"I can help you through wizardry, but in the end you will have to help yourselves. I can give you the means to save Jumbles Wood, but you will have to do the work yourselves."

Old Crow spoke up.

"Do you mean you can give us some great weapon with which we can defeat the Humans?"

The Wizard shook his head. "No, not a weapon. Quite the opposite, in fact. My plan is for you to make friends with the Humans so that they will not want to destroy your homes."

"Make friends! After we've attacked their house and flooded their land!" exclaimed Old Crow. "Just how do we do that?"

A smile crossed the Wizard's tanned face. "Your friend Hammy may be able to answer that question."

He turned to the puzzled guinea pig. "When you lived at the house, the Humans loved you, didn't they?"

"They had an odd way of showing it," snapped Old Crow, before Hammy could even open his mouth. "They kept him prisoner in a cage…"

Hammy hesitated before replying. "I hated being in the cage," he admitted. "But I don't think the Humans realised that. They thought they were giving me a house to live in. And they did feed me well and let me out to run around the garden sometimes.

"I think in their own way they DID love me – particularly the little girl Human they called Mandy. She used to hold me in her arms and stroke my fur which…" he blushed slightly… "was quite, er, pleasant."

Old Crow flapped his wings in disgust. "Nobody has ever stroked me," he said.

Snuff fought to stop himself smiling and thought to himself: "I'm not surprised." But he said nothing.

The Wizard spoke again. "I happen to know that Mandy does love Hammy. She was awfully upset when he escaped. She cried and cried for several days. She searched all over the place for him and persuaded her mother and father to search as well. Even now, although she has managed to stop crying, she hopes that one day he will return."

Snuff had been listening carefully. "So, this little girl, Mandy…she is the Human who may help us?" he asked.

"Yes. She will help because she loves all animals – and Hammy in particular."

Old Crow was his usual crotchety self. "I don't see how a little girl can help us if the other Humans are against it."

"Trust me," smiled the Wizard. "It is quite amazing what little girls can do."

Blink Otter had been taking no part in the conversation but had been listening intently, his eyes blinking at varying speeds depending on what was being said. Finally he said: "Even if this little girl can help us, how do we talk to her?"

"That is where the wizardry comes in. I can create a magic potion which, when taken by any animal, will let them talk to any Human who really loves them. Then it will be up to you to do the rest – and that will mean Hammy will have to return to the Human house."

The guinea pig nodded. "I had already worked that out for myself," he said. "I am the only one of us that Mandy knows. I am the one she will listen to – if I am able to talk to her in her language."

"You will be able to, after you have taken my potion. But the effect wears off after a week, so you will not have to waste time."

"Would it be a good idea if we all went to see this little girl – and all took the language potion?" asked Snuff.

"That is a matter for you" replied the Wizard. "I can certainly make enough potion for you all. But as I have said before, I can only give you the means. You must do the rest yourself."

The Wizard looked up at the sky. The sun was sinking fast and the woodland around his clearing was taking on a dark, gloomy look.

"It will soon be night," he said. "You are a long way from home and it will take me some time to prepare the potion. I suggest we sample that crab-apple and blackcurrant pie now and that you sleep in my cave tonight.

"Then, in the morning, I can prepare the potion while you have a good porridge breakfast to prepare you for the journey home."

Four heads nodded in agreement. All four were feeling ready for bed after what had been an eventful day. All four were ready to sample more of the Wizard's cooking – and none fancied journeying home in the dark.

But Snuff suddenly thought of something that had been worrying him.

"Mr Wizard. You did mention earlier that your plan might involve a great sacrifice. What did you mean?"

The Wizard nodded gravely. "Yes," he said, slowly. "It could do. It is just possible that the little girl, Mandy, might be so pleased to see Hammy again that she will want him to stay with her forever.

"Even if the plan works, and she agrees to help save Jumbles Wood, she might still want Hammy to return to live at the Human house. It is even possible that she will want the rest of you to stay there too. It may be necessary for you to give up your freedom in return for saving the wood."

The four friends looked at each other as the Wizard's words sank in. Then Hammy said: "That is a chance I am prepared to take – but I would not expect any of the rest of you to come with me."

Snuff said: "I think it is a chance we may all have to take." Blink nodded – and even Old Crow muttered agreement.

"If Jumbles Wood is destroyed we will have no homes anyway," he said.

"Right," said the Wizard. "Let's have that pie."

CHAPTER 16

The magic potion

Next morning, the four friends awoke, refreshed and with pleasant memories of the delicious crab-apple and blackcurrant pie they had demolished the night before. The Wizard had clearly been up and about for some time for a large fire was burning in front of the cave, with two cooking pots steaming on it.

The larger of the two contained porridge, while the second contained a bubbling, dark green brew, the nature of which the animals could only guess.

"I hope you all slept well," said the Wizard, appearing from behind a nearby tree with an armful of nuts and berries which he tossed into the smaller cooking pot.

"Very well, thank you," said Snuff, on behalf of all four.

The Wizard motioned to four rocks around the fire and soon they were all seated enjoying quite the most tasty porridge they had ever tasted.

"A secret recipe," explained the Wizard. "You won't get porridge like that anywhere else."

Old Crow eyed the other cooking pot. "Is that the magic language potion?" he asked.

"Yes, indeed. It is nearly ready. It is also a secret recipe, made from various things which grow in the wood. At the moment it would not taste very nice and it wouldn't work. But when it has been simmering for a certain time, I bring it to the boil and use one of my spells – which are also secret – to give it magical properties.

"It will be ready by the time we have finished breakfast."

Sure enough, by the time the four friends had finished eating, the dark, bubbling mixture in the smaller pot was beginning to reach boiling point. The animals watched, fascinated, as the Wizard disappeared into his cave to emerge a few moments later carrying a wand and wearing a tall, pointed hat.

"Ah – now he looks more like a wizard," whispered Old Crow.

The Wizard began to caper around the fire, occasionally waving the wand over the bubbling contents of the pot and muttering strange words. Suddenly a green froth appeared on top of the liquid, there was a loud bang and a cloud of green steam rose into the air. Almost immediately, the liquid stopped bubbling.

"There – it's ready," said the Wizard. "The green smoke arises from the fact that all the ingredients are green and grow in the wood. That's why they call me the Green Wizard."

He paused and then added: "Have you decided how many of you want to take the potion? I have made enough for all."

The four members of the Animal Council had, in fact, discussed this before going to sleep the night before and had decided they would all take the magic potion.

Snuff said: "We don't know if we'll all need it, but we think it best if all of us have the power to speak to the human girl, just in case it comes in useful."

The Wizard nodded agreement.

"A wise decision," he said. "But come – the potion must be taken immediately if it is to be effective."

The animals queued while the Wizard spooned the now bright green liquid into their mouths, muttering a few more strange words as he did so. It tasted little different to water – but each of them felt a strange glow as they swallowed the potion.

"How long before it starts to work?" asked Old Crow.

"It is working already," said the Wizard. "You can tell what I am saying, can't you?"

"Yes," said Old Crow, a trifle irritably. "But I could tell what you were saying before."

The Wizard laughed. "That was because I was speaking YOUR language. Now I am using Human speech – although I have to admit I am a bit out of practice these days."

It was all rather puzzling for the four friends, but they had no choice but to believe the Wizard as there were no other Humans around to test their new skill on.

In any case, there was no time to waste if they were to return home, report to Brigadier Fox and make plans to return to the human house before the magic potion wore off.

They thanked the Wizard, said their goodbyes and set off on the journey home. Snuff turned to take a last look at The Wizard waving from the entrance to his cave.

"I wonder if we'll ever meet him again," he said.

CHAPTER 17

A walk in the wood

Amanda crept down the stairs, trying to be as quiet as possible. She carefully stepped over the third stair because she knew it always creaked.

It was early morning and the sun had just risen. Father and Mother were still asleep in bed and so was Robin. Normally, Amanda would have still been asleep as well.

But today she had decided she just had to do one more thing to try and find Hammy. Father and Mother had searched all around the house. Robin had repeatedly gone off with Max, hoping he might find the little guinea pig in the fields and along the lane. Even father's workmen had looked around the building site, in case Hammy was hiding there.

Amanda herself had spent many hours searching..

But no-one had ventured into Jumbles Wood.

Amanda knew her parents would not allow her to go into the wood on her own. When she had suggested they all go and search the wood they had said it was hopeless. Jumbles Wood was just what its name suggested – a jumble of trees, bushes, long grass and prickly thorns. Searching for Hammy there would be like looking for a needle in a haystack, said Father.

Besides, it was quite a long way for such a small animal to go, he added.

But Amanda was not convinced. Jumbles Wood was the only place left to search and she would not be happy until she had been and looked for herself. The best time to go, she decided, would be while everyone else was still in bed.

In the kitchen, Amanda tip-toed to the back door in her stocking feet. She quietly turned the key in the lock and then put on her shoes. Inch by inch she slowly opened the door, making sure it did not squeak.

She was just about to sneak out of the door when she was startled by a quiet voice behind her.

"And just what do you think you are up to, Mandy?"

It was Robin, hands on hips, standing by the kitchen door, a faint smile on his lips.

Jumbles Wood

"I thought we'd got burglars for a moment," he said. "Then I realised it was you. But where do you think you are going?"

"Ssssshhhh!" Mandy held her finger to her lips.

"Don't wake Mum and Dad or we'll be in trouble."

"We? I won't be in trouble – it's not me that is sneaking out of the house. YOU will be in trouble – not me. Anyway, I'll ask you again. Where are you going?"

"Jumbles Wood – to try and find Hammy."

"What! Mum and Dad would have a fit! You know they wouldn't let you go on your own."

"Of course I do – that's why I'm going while they are still asleep."

"Well you're not. It isn't safe. I'm going to wake them up."

"You mustn't," hissed Amanda. " I'll never forgive you if you do."

Robin hesitated. He could see his sister was determined and he understood why. But he knew he could not let her go into the wood on her own. He made a quick decision.

"Well, OK. But I'm coming with you and we'll take Max as well. We stand a better chance of finding him if we take Max. He's a good tracker.

"And we must leave a note for Mum and Dad, just in case they wake up and wonder where we are."

Amanda nodded. She realised what Robin was saying made sense – and she also knew that if she didn't agree her brother would probably wake their parents.

Robin got the dog's lead and they tip-toed out of the back door. Max was somewhat surprised to be aroused so early in the morning, but Robin managed to wake him quietly.

Once out of the garden, they no longer needed to be quiet.

"We must as quick as we can," said Robin. "If Mum and Dad wake up and find us both missing we'll really be trouble – both of us."

The pair hurried across the fields towards Jumbles Wood, Robin and Max leading the way. They had to climb a couple of fences and cross a stream, using stepping stones. Soon they were entering the wood.

At first the trees were thinly scattered and not very tall. But as they hurried on, the trees got bigger and undergrowth crowded in around them.

There was no sign of a path to follow and frequently they had to duck down low to get under overhanging branches.

"It's quite spooky," said Amanda. "I didn't realize it would be so dark under the trees."

"Well think about what it would have been like on your own," said Robin. "At least you've got Max and I to protect you."

Amanda didn't reply – but stuck her tongue out at her brother behind his back.

On they went, pressing further into the wood. Above them, they could see birds perched in the trees, but there was no sign of any animals on the ground at all. Certainly no sign of a lost guinea pig.

"I think we are wasting our time," said Robin. "We'll have to turn back soon, or Mum and Dad will find out we're missing."

"Just a few minutes more," insisted Amanda. "I feel, somehow, as if we are being watched. As if there are lot of eyes looking through the leaves."

"You are probably right. There must be hundreds of creatures living in this wood, but they won't let us see them."

Suddenly they came upon a small clearing. A shaft of light had penetrated the canopy of leaves above and was bathing one corner of the clearing in the warm, morning sunshine.

Robin stopped and pointed. "Look Mandy…just look at that."

There, fast asleep on a pile of leaves close to a hole in the ground, was a badger.

Amanda's eyes widened. "Isn't he gorgeous! And he's snoring!"

The pair stared in fascination as the badger stirred slightly in his sleep, scratched himself on the nose and continued to gently snore.

Robin had wisely clamped a hand over Max's mouth to make sure he didn't bark. But the big dog could not be kept silent for long. He had probably never seen a badger before and the sight of one so obviously enjoying a snooze in the sun, when he, Max, had so recently been aroused from his own slumber, was one he could not endure for long.

He wriggled in Robin's grasp, pulled hard on the lead and finally managed to free his mouth from the boy's hand.

"Yooooooowl!"

Jumbles Wood

The sound was not one which Max would normally have owned up to. It was not a bark, nor a howl or even a yelp. Rather, it was a mixture of all three. But it was loud – and it was certainly enough to awake the peacefully sleeping badger.

In mid-snore, the startled animal leapt almost vertically into the air, returned to earth with a bump and disappeared down the hole in the ground. The silence of the woodland was shattered as chattering birds rose from the surrounding trees by the score.

The dog, now thoroughly enraged by what, to him, seemed the completely unreasonable attempts by his master to keep him still and quiet, leapt forward, dragging the boy behind him. It was all Robin could do to hang on to the lead – but hang on he did.

"Max – stop. To heel!" he shouted. And the dog instinctively obeyed. He crouched, glaring down the hole into which the badger had disappeared and growled fiercely. But he stopped pulling on the lead.

"Phew! That was close," gasped Robin. "I thought I'd lost him for a moment."

Amanda was furious.

"I don't know why we brought him. That poor old badger must have had the shock of his life – just when he was enjoying a quiet snooze."

"We brought him because we are supposed to be looking for your guinea pig, not sleepy badgers," retorted Robin.

"Anyway, after all that noise I don't suppose we'll see any more animals of any description. And it's time we turned back. Mum and Dad will be getting up any time now now. We've come a lot further than I had intended and we haven't seen a sign of Hammy. Dad's right – we'll never find him in here."

Amanda could not really argue. She realised they now been away from the house for too long.

In silence they hurried back home. Max was pushed somewhat unwillingly back into his kennel and Robin and Amanda crept back into the house and up to their bedrooms. When their parents awoke a few minutes later it was as if nothing had ever happened.

CHAPTER 18

Persuading the Brigadier

B rigadier Fox thumped his desk with his paw.

"Nonsense," he bellowed. "Absolute nonsense!"

He had just received the report on the expedition to seek help from the Green Wizard. He had heard from all four members of the expedition, of their meeting with the Wizard, their night in his cave and the magic language potion. And he did not like what he had heard.

"You have ALL taken this so-called potion?" he roared, his bushy tail swishing back and to with rage.

Snuff, Hammy, Blink and Old Crow all nodded.

"Then you have all taken leave of your senses," shouted the incensed fox. "You might have been poisoned."

"Well, we weren't," said Old Crow, defiantly.

"But you MIGHT have been," Brigadier Fox barked. "You could have been taking anything."

"His crab-apple and blackcurrant pie was excellent," protested Blink Otter.

"I don't give a hoot for his crab-apple and blackcurrant pie," screamed the fox.

"His porridge was pretty good too," said Hammy.

"But the potion," roared the fox. "What proof have you that it works?"

Snuff tried to stay calm. "Until we go and meet the Human girl, we won't really know. But we had to take the chance. We could speak to the Wizard after taking the potion."

The Brigadier drummed his fingers on the desk. "Apparently, you could speak to him BEFORE you took the potion."

"Yes, but he explained that. He was speaking our language at first, but afterwards he was using Human speech. And we could still understand him."

Brigadier Fox sighed. "How do you know that is true?" he barked. "He could have been, and probably was, making complete fools of you."

"Nothing has been lost, sir," insisted Snuff. "We knew from the start we were taking a bit of a chance in visiting the Wizard. The worst thing that can have happened is that we made a wasted journey.

"But if the potion works…"

The Brigadier rose to his feet and began pacing the room. "This so-called magic language potion may or may not work," he growled. "But the only way to find out is to risk sending my only reliable senior officers into the heart of enemy territory…"

He broke off to glower at the reclining figure of Colonel Badger, who was somehow managing to sleep through the commanding officer's ranting and raving. The glower was wasted, however, as the old badger continued to snooze, unaware of what was going on around him and completely unconcerned at being dismissed as unreliable.

"What you four don't know," the Brigadier continued, "is that while you have been away eating crab apple and blackcurrant pie with this so-called wizard, there have been developments here."

"Developments?" queried Snuff.

"Yes…serious developments about which we know very little – thanks to a certain senior officer being asleep on duty!"

He broke off to glower at the dozing badger.

"What exactly has happened?" asked Snuff.

Brigadier Fox sighed wearily. "Humans have invaded Jumbles Wood – accompanied by a dog. That is what has happened."

He prodded the sleeping badger in the ribs.

"Wake up you old fool," he barked. "Tell your fellow officers what a mess you've made of things while they were away."

Colonel Badger awoke abruptly. "What…that is, why…or how?" he spluttered.

"Tell them," roared the fox, thumping his desk again. "Give your highly detailed report on the invasion by the Humans – the same one you have already given to me."

"Ah, yes. That is, let me see…"began the badger, rubbing sleep from his eyes. "I was on duty in the wood when…"

"You mean you were sleeping in the wood," interrupted the Brigadier.

"Well, I might have just dozed off for a minute," the badger admitted. "It had been a very long day. Anyway, all of a sudden there were these two Humans and a dog – right there in front of me."

"G-g-good grief! – what did you do?" asked Blink Otter.

"Well, I sprang into action immediately," began the badger. But Brigadier Fox could not contain himself.

"You mean you jumped out of your skin and dived into your wretched sett to hide," he barked. "What's more, you were so terrified you can't even remember what happened next."

"Well, it all happened very quickly. I heard the dog howling and saw him charging towards me. I really had no choice but to go to ground. It was a very big dog."

"What sort of Humans were they?" asked Hammy. "I know all the Humans from the house."

"No point in asking him," replied Brigadier Fox, again glaring at the badger. He was too busy saving his own skin. He doesn't even know what sort of Humans they were.

"But fortunately we have reports from various birds in the area and, it would seem they were Human cubs – the boy and the girl from the house."

"Ah, Mandy and her brother," said Hammy. "I wonder what they were doing in the wood?"

"That's obvious," said the Brigadier, his whiskers bristling. "They were on a scouting mission. We have attacked them once and they want to know what sort of forces we have available.

"If a certain so-called senior officer had been awake, we might have been able to make sure they got the wrong sort of information. We might have even captured them. As it is, they've gone away knowing we're asleep at our posts!"

"They didn't seem to be doing any harm," protested Old Badger.

"And how would you know, you old fool?" retorted the fox. "You were fast asleep."

He resumed pacing up and down, frowning.

"The situation we are now in is that we know the Humans are coming into the wood, although we don't know why, our attack on the Human house seems to have been a failure and our only plan to strike back involves me sending my four senior officers into enemy territory to see if some so-called magic potion works of not."

"We don't ALL need to go," Hammy broke in. "Apparently I am the one most likely to be able to persuade Mandy to help us, so I am the only one who needs to go back to the house."

Brigadier Fox was beginning to calm down. His military mind was working busily on the situation as he now saw it.

"You certainly DON'T need to all go," he agreed. "But I think it would be unreasonable for Captain Hammy to go alone. He will need support, and I believe Major Snuff Rabbit and Air Commodore Crow will be sufficient, along with a platoon of moles and some air support.

"I have other plans for Admiral Blink Otter, however."

Blink blinked nervously. "Other plans...?" he queried.

The Brigadier ignored him. "Fortunately," he said, "While you have been away on your hare-brained mission, I have been busy myself – without much help from my so-called second-in-command."   He again glared at Colonel Badger, who was just beginning to nod again..

"I have received valuable intelligence from our airborne reconnaissance missions over and around the human house. This leads me to believe that we could make another, much more effective strike against the enemy.

"This would involve another naval operation, so the admiral will be required for this."

Old Crow raised a questioning wing. "Might we be told about this operation, sir?" he asked. "Seeing as it was MY airborne forces that provided the intelligence."

"Certainly. It has come to our notice that further upstream from where Blink...that is, Admiral...Blink and his team built the last dam, a large tree has fallen across the stream. At present the water is flowing freely beneath it, but it would not require much effort on our part to construct another dam."

"But," said Old Crow, "The last dam didn't cause much of a problem for the Humans. Why should this one?"

"Because," said Brigadier Fox, "this time it would flood the Human house itself – and the road leading to it."

Hammy found himself thinking of the garden where he had once lived. He thought of the little girl, the boy and even Max, the bullying dog. Much as he had been pleased to escape from the place, he did not really like the idea of it being flooded.

Snuff said: "Surely we should be allowed to try the Wizard's plan first?"

The Brigadier sniffed contemptuously. "Yes – but I, for one, do not think it is likely to be successful. Also, I think there is a risk of it going wrong, with all of you being captured. So I want to be ready to strike immediately if necessary.

"I want Admiral Blink and his team in place, ready to block the stream at a moment's notice and I also want squadrons of birds in place ready to bomb the Humans if things get out of hand.

"I realise such an attack is unlikely to be a serious problem to the enemy, but it could keep them occupied while anyone trapped inside the garden fence escaped."

There was no time for argument. Hammy, Snuff and Old Crow knew that the Wizard's potion would only work for a week – if it would work at all. So plans were immediately made for their return to the Human house.

They were only interrupted when a sleepy Colonel Badger suddenly stirred, sat up abruptly and said: "Oh, you're back! How did you get on with the Wizard?"

CHAPTER 18

Talking to the animals

Amanda was helping Mother in the garden. Robin had gone out with Father to take Max for a walk and it was too nice a day to stay indoors. So Mother showed her how to pull up weeds in a flower border. The important thing, Mother said, was to know the difference between weeds and flowers so that you didn't pull up flowers by mistake.

Once she was satisfied that Amanda would not pull up any flowers, Mother went off to work at the other end of the garden.

Amanda concentrated very hard while she was working, not just to make sure she did not mistake flowers for weeds, but also so that she would not keep seeing the little hutch where her guinea pig used to live. She could think about Hammy now without crying, but it still upset her to see the empty hutch. She still hoped that one day her little pet would return home.

She was concentrating so hard on her weeding that when a voice suddenly said: "Are you Mandy?" she didn't really take any notice. But when the voice said: "Are you Mandy?" a second time, she looked up, surprised.

There was no-one there. Mother was at the other end of the garden, bending over a flower bed, with her back to her. There was no sign of Robin and Father coming back with Max. The garden was completely empty. Except, that is, for a large, black bird, perched on the fence.

Amanda stared at the bird, which stared back at her. She was about to turn back to the border when the bird suddenly raised itself to its full height, flapped its wings and distinctly said in a rather irritated voice: "I said, are you Mandy?"

For a moment, Amanda was too shocked to do anything. She didn't quite know whether to scream with fright or burst out laughing. She just stared in amazement at the black bird.

"I can't go on repeating myself," said the bird, this time sounding extremely cross. "But are you Mandy?"

Amanda found her voice at last. "You're talking!" she exclaimed. "You're talking – but birds don't talk!"

"This one does," said the bird, and flapped his wings again. "In fact, ALL birds do. It's just that, usually, YOU can't understand them."

There could be no doubt about it now. The big, black bird sitting on the garden fence WAS talking to her. She could see his beak opening and closing as he spoke.

Suddenly, Amanda felt a little frightened. She knew birds did not usually hurt people – even quite big birds. But then, they didn't usually talk either. Amanda felt she had to call Mother.

She ran up the garden calling "Mum, Mum – there's a talking bird in the garden."

"Drat it!" exclaimed Old Crow. "This isn't getting things off to a very good start at all."

He shouted: "Wait – come back…I can explain…" But the little girl was too busy running and shouting to her mother and didn't hear him.

Mother turned to see what all the commotion was about. "What's the matter, Mandy? What are you talking about?"

Amanda pointed at the bird sitting on the fence.

"That bird, Mum. It spoke to me."

"Don't be silly, dear. It's only a crow."

Old Crow let out a shriek of indignation. "What do you mean, ONLY a crow?" he shouted. "I'm a Jackdaw – prince of the crows."

"There you are, Mum – it spoke again."

Mother stared at her daughter. "It made a peculiar noise, I'll grant you that," she said. "But crows don't talk. The only birds that can talk are parrots – and even they have to be taught how to say a few words. They don't really know what they are saying."

"But it used my name – it asked me if I was Mandy," Amanda persisted.

Old Crow said: "You are wasting your time, Mandy. Your mother doesn't understand what I am saying. Only YOU can understand me. But there's no need to worry – I'm a friend and I have come to help you. If you had only admitted you were Mandy when I first asked, we needn't have had all this commotion."

Amanda stared at the bird and then at Mother. "It's talking to me, Mum, honest."

She turned back to the bird. "Well, yes, I am Mandy, if you must know. But what do you want?"

Jumbles Wood

"I've got important news – and I have brought an old friend of yours to see you," said Old Crow.

Jane Watson stared at her daughter. "Is he frightening you? Do you want me to shoo him away?" she asked.

Amanda shook her head. "No – I'm not frightened. But he is talking to me and…well, it's strange."

Jane Watson looked at the bird. He wasn't doing any harm, she decided, and he appeared to be amusing Mandy. She was obviously playing some sort of game and the strange black bird was part of it.

"All right – you carry on talking to your bird and I'll carry on with my gardening," she said, turning back to the flower bed.

"Right, that's settled," said Old Crow, hopping along the top of the fence. "Now perhaps we can get down to business."

Amanda was still puzzled. "Why can I understand what you are saying when Mum can't?" she asked.

Old Crow shrugged his shoulders. "I'm not too sure about that myself," he admitted. "Apparently I can only talk to humans who love animals."

"But Mum loves animals."

"Well, she can't love them enough. That's the only thing I can think of. You've got to really, really love animals to be able to talk to them. Like the way you love Hammy, I suppose."

"Hammy? What do you know about Hammy?" The mention of her missing pet made Amanda forget all about how odd it was to be talking to a bird.

"He's my friend – and I've brought him to see you,"

"Hammy is with you? Where is he? Oh please show me where he is."

Old Crow motioned to the far end of the garden – well away from where Amanda's mother was working.

"Follow me – but be prepared for a surprise."

"He's not hurt, is he? "

"No. He's never been in better health. But…well I'll let him tell you himself."

"You mean I'll be able to talk to Hammy as well?"

"You will if you love him enough – and from what I've heard, there's not much doubt about that."

Jumbles Wood

Old Crow hopped along the top of the fence, making sure that Amanda was following in the garden below. He knew that Snuff Rabbit and a willing platoon of moles from the Jumbles Wood Army had been busy digging a new tunnel into the garden and that by now Hammy would be inside the garden, hiding behind a bush.

When Amanda saw her long-lost pet she cried with joy. She picked him up, held him close to her and rubbed his furry face gently against her own.

"Oh, Hammy, it's you, it's really you," she repeatedly cried.

"Yes, it's me," the guinea pig replied. "But have a care, Mandy. I'm only little, you know."

Old Crow remained on the fence, viewing the reunion with considerable disdain. But Snuff Rabbit, who had accompanied Hammy into the garden, stood a short distance away watching with some envy. He had never realised before how much a Human could love an animal.

Suddenly Amanda noticed him and, before Snuff could even blink, had him in her arms as well.

"Oh," she cried. "A lovely rabbit as well...where have you come from?"

The answer to that question formed the start of a very long story, as Hammy and Snuff, with occasional irritable interruptions from the watching Old Crow, told the girl of everything that had happened since Hammy had escaped from his hutch.

Amanda's eyes widened and widened as she heard of the efforts of the Jumbles Wood animals to protect their homes, the raid on the garden, the flooding of the building site and the long journey to seek help from the Green Wizard.

"I've heard people talk about him," she said. "My Dad thinks he is just an old tramp who lives in the wood."

Occasionally, Mother would call from the other end of the garden: "Are you all right, Mandy?"

But all Amanda had to do was shout back: "Yes, Mum," and they were left undisturbed.

Old Crow let the two furry folk do most of the talking, but he did have one pointed question for the girl.

"Why did you and your brother and the dog come into the wood yesterday?" he asked.

Jumbles Wood

Amanda was surprised.

"You mean you saw us?" she exclaimed.

"Watched you every step of the way," said Old Crow, exaggerating somewhat.

"Well, we were only looking for Hammy," said Amanda. "It was the only place my Mum and Dad hadn't looked. But we didn't see anything except an old badger sleeping in the sun."

Snuff smiled. "You gave him a bit of a shock, I believe."

"Yes – but it was an accident. Max gets a bit excited over things like that. We didn't mean to hurt any animals. I love animals and would never hurt them."

Hammy, who was secretly rather enjoying being stroked and cuddled by the girl, said: "The question is, can you help us?"

"More to the point," cackled Old Crow, "WILL you help us?"

Amanda frowned. "Of course I WANT to help you," she said. "And I WILL do everything I can to help you. But I don't really know what I can do."

Snuff said: "The Wizard seemed to think you could help."

"I know, but it's my Dad who wants to build the houses. I've never wanted him to do it – and neither has Mum. We think it would spoil the countryside. In fact, in some ways we wish he hadn't even built our own house.

"But that's what he does – he's a builder. He doesn't want to harm animals and he doesn't think he is spoiling the countryside. He just wants to build houses."

"The trouble is," said Hammy, "It is difficult for him to do one without doing the other."

At the other end of the garden, Jane Watson finished working on her flower border. She looked up and down but there was no sign of Amanda.

"What is that girl doing?" she said to herself. "Everything has been too quiet for too long."

She walked down the garden, looking behind shrubs and bushes, but there was no sign of the girl.

"Where are you, Mandy?"

There was no reply – but Mother thought she saw a movement behind a large bush – a splash of blue the same colour as Amanda's blouse.

She bent to get under the spreading branches of a cherry tree, rounded a corner and saw Amanda sitting on the ground holding something small and furry in her arms.

"So there you are…and…Good Heavens! Is that Hammy?"

"It is Mum – he's come back to us."

"Well I am pleased – I told you he might come back. I don't know, talking birds and now Hammy is back. Aren't you a lucky girl!"

"Yes. It's wonderful. Hammy has been talking to me too – and so has Snuff Rabbit!"

"Who? Oh yes…" Mother caught sight of Snuff, who, when the woman arrived, had cautiously moved closer to the tunnel entrance through which he and Hammy had entered the garden.

"I don't know whether your father will be so pleased to have wild rabbits in the garden. They eat the plants, you know. Perhaps we should let him go and you should put Hammy back in his hutch where he will be safe."

"No, Mum. Hammy doesn't like the hutch. He has told me. He feels like a prisoner in it."

"Well I don't think we can let him roam around the garden, dear. Max might have him for his breakfast."

Mother leaned over and stroked Hammy on the head.

"He is very cuddly and cute," she said. "It would be a pity if you lost him again. He would be much safer in the hutch."

"No I would not," squeaked Hammy, indignantly.

Mother laughed: "I wonder what he is trying to tell us – it's almost as if he was talking."

"He IS talking, Mum. He's saying he doesn't want to go back in the hutch."

Hammy looked at Amanda. "I think your Mum NEARLY understands what I am saying," he said. "But please don't let her put me back in the hutch.

"I promise I will come back and talk again tomorrow if you let me go. And I am sure Snuff will come too."

Snuff, who had edged even closer to the tunnel, said: "Yes – I'll be here."

Amanda put Hammy down on the ground.

"I'm letting him go," she said. "He has promised to come back tomorrow and I believe he will."

Jumbles Wood

Mother sighed. "Well, don't come crying to me if he doesn't," she said. "I don't know what Dad would say if he thought you were talking to birds and animals. I expect he'd think you were crackers."

Amanda wasn't listening to her. She was watching Hammy and Snuff disappear into the tunnel, waving as they both turned at the entrance to look back.

"See you tomorrow," she called.

Mother smiled. "Well, if they come back, I'll begin to believe you really can talk to them," she said.

That night, after Amanda and Robin had both gone to bed, Jane Watson told her husband what had happened.

"She thinks she can talk to animals and birds – do you think it's is something for us to be worrying about?"

Harry Watson frowned. "It might be. But it's more likely some fantasy children's game she is playing. Remarkable that the little guinea pig came back, though. Quite remarkable. But it will be even more remarkable if he comes back again."

CHAPTER 19

A jealous crow

Safely back at Snuff's Oak, Snuff, Hammy and Old Crow made the usual report to Brigadier Fox.

The most important point, so far as the brigadier was concerned, was that the magic language potion worked. They COULD talk to the Human girl. But Snuff and Hammy were also convinced that they had made a friend of Amanda and that she would help them.

"When we return tomorrow, we should find out if Mandy has thought of a way of helping us," said Hammy. "She definitely was pleased to see me – and she didn't try to keep me in the hutch.

"She is definitely an animal lover – the Wizard said only true animal lovers would be able to talk with us and she was able to understand everything I said. It was wonderful, being able to talk with a Human."

Old Crow, as usual, looked on the black side of things.

"The mother was the problem," he said. "I was worried a few times – particularly when she tried to persuade the girl to put Hammy in the hutch. When she reached out to stroke him I was ready to call in an air strike immediately – I had a squadron of sparrow hawks ready on the house roof."

"Well I'm glad you didn't," said Hammy. "I think the mother could prove to be a friend. I thought she ALMOST understood what I said at one time. I thought that perhaps she was NEARLY a true animal lover and that with a bit of effort she might be able to speak to us."

He paused and added: "It was quite pleasant when she stroked me."

Old Crow snorted. "Pah! I don't know what it is you furry fellows see in being stroked – I couldn't stand it.

"But you two – it was sickening! It was bad enough having the girl pick you up and stroke you, but you even had her mother fawning over you and treating you like a pair of cuddly toys. I found it quite disgusting!"

Brigadier Fox had, unusually for him, been listening in silence. But now he snapped: "You're just jealous, Old Crow, because no-one would ever want to stroke you. I'm a little furry myself and while most folk are too frightened of me to want to stroke me, I do remember that as a cub it was quite a pleasant experience."

A sullen Old Crow said: "Hmmmmph!"

"Overall," the brigadier went on, "I think it has been a successful operation and, hopefully, tomorrow you will make more progress.

"But I'm disappointed you don't have more information about enemy troop deployment, garrison strength, etc. I've not heard a word yet about the soldiers in the enemy headquarters."

Hammy laughed. "That's because there aren't any – they are just toys belonging to Mandy's brother, Robin.

"He likes playing war games in the garden – and we mistook his toy soldiers, tanks and forts for real ones.

"The threat to Jumbles Wood isn't from a military invasion – it's just from Humans building houses and roads for themselves."

Brigadier Fox's whiskers bristled. It wasn't easy for a military man, a veteran of numerous campaigns and the commander in chief of the Jumbles Wood Army to accept that he had been waging war against a toy army. It wasn't easy, so he was having none of it.

"Nonsense!" he exclaimed. "You don't think I'd be sending my troops into battle against toys, do you?"

"Well, Mandy says they are just toys."

"It could be a trick – a cunning plan to put us off our guard.

"We must stay on full alert and be ready to resume military action if necessary. Blink Otter and his team have made good progress in preparing another dam. I have been out and examined the area myself and am quite sure we can, if necessary, create a deluge which would really flood the Human house.

"If this Mandy girl proves to be our friend and can do something to help we need do nothing – but if not, we are ready."

Snuff said: "The REAL problem may be the father. He's the one who wants to build houses and roads and he is the head of the Human family. I am afraid it may take a lot to stop him – whether or not the soldiers are toys."

A grumpy Old Crow, who had still not got over the way furry animals got stroked and cuddled, again said: "Hmmmmmph!"

He added: "The soldiers may be toys, but at least they don't get stroked!"

CHAPTER 20

Max meets his match

Next morning, bright and early, Old Crow led his squadron of sparrow hawks back to the Human house. They took up positions on the roof, as on the previous day, while Old Crow himself perched on the garden fence and waited.

He took particular notice that Max, the dog, who had been out for a walk the previous day, was now snoozing in his kennel. Old Crow noted with some relief that the dog was attached to a chain

Hammy and Snuff, of course, took longer to make the journey from Snuff's Oak but by the time Amanda emerged from the house they were ready to go through the tunnel into the garden. They were encouraged to find that, unlike the tunnels that had been dug at the time of the raid, this one had not been filled in.

Amanda walked straight up to Old Crow and took him by surprise by holding out her hand.

"Hello, Old Crow," she said. "You may perch on my hand, if you like."

"Oh, well...that is...I don't usually perch on people," he stuttered. "In fact, I have never been asked to perch on anyone before."

"It's up to you," said Amanda, still holding out her hand. "I'm just trying to be friends. You are quite a handsome bird, really."

"I am?" Old Crow was taken aback by the rare compliment.

"Yes. You have beautiful black feathers – and I like the grey bits on your neck and the back of your head. I can see why a Jackdaw is the prince of all crows."

"Oh, well..." Old Crow hesitated. "I still won't...er...perch, if you don't mind. But that doesn't mean I don't want to be friends."

Jumbles Wood

"OK – that's all right with me," laughed Amanda. "But where are Hammy and Snuff?"

The girl seemed to have quite overcome the shock of being able to talk to birds and animals and was chatting naturally, just as if she would was chatting to a Human friend.

Old Crow motioned to the large bush behind which Amanda had spent most of the time while talking to her new animal friends the previous day. The girl bobbed under the branches of the cherry tree and settled on the ground next to the tunnel. Her face lit up as first Hammy and then Snuff emerged into the daylight.

"You've come back, just as you promised," she cried.

"Of course," said Hammy. "We don't break our promises. In any case, we have serious matters to discuss."

Amanda became more serious. "I know," she said. "I have lain awake most of the night, thinking about it. I want to help, but I don't know how I can.

"I heard Mum and Dad talking after I had gone to bed and they think I am playing some sort of game – imagining that I can talk to animals. They just don't believe it.

"But they also didn't believe you would come back today, Hammy, so they have been proved wrong about that already."

Hammy sighed. "The trouble is, our leader, Brigadier Fox, has difficulty in believing in things as well. He has given us time to try and make friends with you, but he has his doubts about the whole idea that you can, or will, help us. He's rather impatient, you see, and he's got plans for another attack on you if we fail.

"I know the first attack didn't bother you very much – but the Brigadier thinks his next one will cause much more damage."

Hammy wanted to tell Amanda about the plan to flood the house but he was under orders from Brigadier Fox not to do so. "Military secret," the Brigadier had said. "Vital that it remains top secret."

Amanda said: "I think the first thing I have to do is get Mum on my side. We must let her see that you have come back today, just like I told them you would. Dad's at work, but Mum will tell him when he gets home.

"I don't think we'll ever get them to believe I can talk to you all – and when the Wizard's spell wears off I won't be able to. But I'm sure we can all still be friends even when we can't talk."

"Of course we can," said Hammy. "I think I can speak for all the animals of Jumbles Wood, when I say that you, Mandy, will always be our friend. But if you cannot help us, somehow, there may soon be no animals in Jumbles Wood – and no Jumbles Wood at all."

The girl reached out and stroked Hammy's furry head and a tear rolled down her cheek. "I love you all – even the ones I have never seen," she said, softly.

She looked up at Old Crow, still perched on the fence. "I even love you, Old Crow, even if you are a bit crotchety."

If he hadn't been so black, Old Crow would have blushed.

Then Amanda brushed away her tears and stood up. "We must get started immediately. You must come into the garden – right in the middle of the lawn – so that Mum can see you have kept your promise and come back."

Old Crow had been speechless since Amanda had said she loved him. He could not remember anyone ever saying they loved him and he had been thinking deeply about the peculiar feeling he had got inside when Amanda had offered to let him perch on her hand.

He had found himself feeling that it WOULD be rather nice to sit on her hand and let her stroke his black feathers.

But then he pulled himself up sharply. He must be going soft in his old age. And a sudden thought had occurred to him.

"What about the dog?" he said. "He's not very keen on rabbits and guinea pigs wandering around his garden."

"Max? He's chained up in his kennel," said Amanda. "His bark is worse than his bite, you know. He'll probably make a lot of noise, but as long as we keep well away from the kennel he won't be able to do anything.

"With a bit of luck, he won't even know what's going on."

So it was that Hammy and Snuff marched smartly out onto the lawn as Amanda led her mother from the kitchen. Old Crow, meanwhile, fluttered importantly along the top of the fence, keeping a keen eye on the dog kennel.

"My Goodness," exclaimed Mother. "You were right, Mandy – Hammy has come back again – and brought that rabbit with him."

"I told you they'd be back, Mum. They made a promise – and animals don't break promises." Mother frowned. She had begun to think Amanda had forgotten about her "talking to the animals" experience. She had not mentioned it at breakfast – and neither had Amanda. But now she was talking about animals' promises – and what's more the animals were there.

Amanda knelt down on the lawn between Hammy and Snuff and began stroking them both.

Hammy said: "From the look on her face, your Mum just doesn't know what to think."

Mother knelt down herself, in front of the two animals and reached out to gently stroke Snuff on the top of his head. Snuff's natural instinct was to bolt – but he managed to sit still and let the Human's hand tickle his furry top and gentle stroke his ears.

"He's awfully tame, Mandy," said Mother. "I think he must be someone's pet who has run away – just like Hammy did."

"No I'm not," said Snuff, somewhat indignantly. "I live in Jumbles Wood in my own house."

Mother pulled her hand away quickly, startled by the rabbit's reaction.

"Do you know, Mandy, it's almost as if he IS trying to talk to me."

"He IS, Mum. He said he's not someone's pet – he lives in his own house in Jumbles Wood."

Just what would have happened next was not clear. Jane Watson was trying desperately to find for herself, an explanation for the animals' behaviour. A voice inside her was telling her she must be dreaming or crazy – but another was urging her to believe what her daughter was telling her. That the animals could talk!

But at that instant Max awoke, sniffed the cool morning air and sensed something strange going on. He looked out of the kennel, saw the rabbit and the guinea pig and leapt to his feet with a roar.

Snuff and Hammy fled as the huge dog sprang from the kennel. Amanda and her mother jumped to their feet and Mother shouted: "Down, Max." But the dog could only see the two fleeing furry figures and he recognised one as the strange little creature with no tail who had made him feel something of a fool on a previous occasion.

Max lunged forward and the chain, which had failed to hold the incensed dog once before, failed again. It snapped, allowing the dog to storm across the lawn.

Jumbles Wood

Jane Watson shouted "STOP!" and threw herself into the dog's path. But Max was big and strong and his speed, combined with his weight, was too much for her. She was bowled over backwards as the dog sped on like an express train.

Hammy and Snuff were by now half-way towards the safety of their tunnel – but Max was gaining on them in leaps and bounds.

Up on the garden fence, Old Crow screeched an order and suddenly the sky was full of beating wings. The sparrow hawks swooped down from the house roof. Wave after wave of birds in orderly, disciplined ranks, dived on the charging dog.

Just how much of what followed was down to luck, and just how much to the strict training the Air Commodore had imposed on the Jumbles Wood Air Force, was something Old Crow was prepared to argue about for years to come.

The sparrow hawk is a bird designed for speed and agility and is capable of carrying an object of its own weight in its claws. It normally hunts alone – so the sight of row after row of them descending on him might well have unnerved the charging dog.

Max hesitated and slowed his pace – and that was his undoing.

For as he slowed, he became an easier target, and Old Crow's airforce had spent hours practicing the art of bombing. With so many birds releasing so many missiles, some had to find their target. And the object that struck Max right on the end of his nose was a large, prickly horse chestnut. It hurt!

Max howled, turned on his heel and raced back to his kennel where he cowered inside, trying desperate to lick his wounded nose.

As quickly as it appeared, the squadron of sparrow hawks vanished and peace and quiet returned to the garden.

Mother picked herself up, brushed herself down and stared around a lawn littered with horse chestnuts, pine cones and acorns.

Amanda had thrown herself to the ground as the massed ranks of birds dived over the garden, although she need not have bothered. The shower of missiles had fallen well clear of her.

Now she stood up and took hold of her mother's hand.

"Well, I never," said Mother. "I have never seen anything like it. Where did all those birds come from? And what's happened to Hammy – and that rabbit?"

"I think they ran back into their little tunnel," said Amanda. "Max is a pest – I don't suppose we'll see them again now and it's all his fault."

Jumbles Wood

A familiar voice cut in and Amanda looked round to see Old Crow perched on the fence.

"You will see them again, " he said. "Sorry about that – but your dog is a bit of a problem for rabbits and guinea pigs, you know. He had to be stopped – but I don't think he is seriously hurt. More a question of hurt pride, I think."

Amanda walked over to the crow and held her hand out again. "I still want to be friends," she said.

Old Crow cackled. "So do I – but I don't think I'll sit on your hand while your mother is watching, if you don't mind. Perhaps another time."

With that he flapped his wings, swooped off the fence and flew off. Amanda heard his croaky voice drifting through the air.

"See you tomorrow."

Jane Watson looked at her daughter.

"You still think you can talk to animals, don't you?"

"I can, Mum. But it's only to the end of the week – the Wizard says so."

"The Wizard? You don't mean that old man who lives in the wood, do you? You've not been to see him?"

"No, of course I haven't. But Hammy has, and Old Crow and Snuff Rabbit. And Blink Otter too – we haven't met him yet, but he's part of the team."

"What team do you mean, Mandy?"

"The team of animals trying to save Jumbles Wood from Dad's houses. They don't want him to build any more because it means they will lose their own homes."

"Ah…is that what this all about? You don't want Dad to build in the wood."

"You know I don't. And I don't think you want him to either. But it's not you and I that matter – it's the animals. They live in Jumbles Wood and they are frightened they are going to lose their homes and everything. They think Jumbles Wood will become like Green Valley – just another village."

"So you've made up this story about talking to the animals, have you? To try and persuade your father not to carry on building."

Jane Watson was relieved, in a way. She could see why Amanda might come up with such a story. In fact, she thought, for a child of her age it was quite an ingenious plan.   She wasn't too happy about her telling tales, but at least it was for a good cause and it was better than having a daughter who needed to see a psychiatrist!

But her feelings of relief were short-lived.

Amanda turned to her and said sharply: "Mum – I haven't made up any stories.

"Honestly – I CAN talk to the animals."

Jumbles Wood

CHAPTER 21

Kisses for father

When Harry Watson came home that evening he and his wife had a hurried, whispered conversation in the hall. Then he went straight to Amanda's bedroom.

"Now then, young lady," he said. "What has been going on today? You have got your mother very worried about you."

Amanda looked up from her chair by the window where she had been reading.

"There's no need to worry about me, Dad. I've explained everything I can to Mum. But if you won't believe me about talking to animals, there is nothing else I can do. You just think I am making things up."

Father sat on the edge of Amanda's bed. "Well, people just CAN'T talk to animals, Mandy. We're not angry with you. We are always ready to talk to you and help you with any problems you have got. But, really, you can't expect us to believe you are talking to a guinea pig, a rabbit and a crow."

"I wouldn't have believed it myself a couple of days ago, Dad. But it's happening. And Hammy came back, just as he said he would. You know that's true, because Mum saw him. And the rabbit – he came back as well…and the crow."

Father frowned. "I will admit that is quite remarkable," he said. "I don't pretend to be able to explain it – but it's still a bit different to animals talking."

He held his arms out and Amanda jumped up from her chair, ran across the room, jumped on his knee and put her arms around his neck.

"Oh, Mandy, your Mum and I do love you so much. You'll always be our little girl and we'll do anything for you."

Amanda kissed her father on the cheek and said softly in his ear: "If you love me and you'll do anything for me, why won't you stop building your houses."

"But Mandy, that's how I make my living. If I don't build houses we won't have any money."

"You could build them somewhere else."

Jumbles Wood

Father looked at her seriously. "Yes, I could build them somewhere else and I will be building more houses in other places as well. But I never knew you felt so strongly about me building these houses."

"I just don't want you to destroy Jumbles Wood."

"But it's not much of a wood, is it? And I wouldn't be using all of it."

Amanda got off her father's knee and walked across to the window to look towards Jumbles Wood.

"You may not think it is much of a wood," she said. "But to the animals who live there it is their home. You have no idea how they feel. How would you like it if someone came and knocked our house down?"

"Well, I wouldn't like it. But I'm not planning to knock any houses down. There would be some trees to fell and bushes to root out – but I'm sure the animals who live there would soon find somewhere else to go."

"That's not what they tell me," Amanda replied.

There was a silence while Father thought things over. No matter what he said, Mandy was persisting with her story about talking animals, he thought.

Finally he said: "Well, as you know, we have already put the foundations in for the next house – the one that will be next door to us.

"How would you feel if I just built that house and didn't build any more? That would mean there was still quite a big field between the houses and the wood – and Jumbles Wood would not be affected at all."

Amanda ran back and threw her arms around her father's neck again. "I would like that a lot," she said. "And I think the animals would like it too."

"Well, I'm not promising anything," her father said, thoughtfully. "But I will think about it. I might just be able to do that – and save your precious wood."

Amanda planted another huge kiss on her father's face.

CHAPTER 22

Flood alert

Brigadier Fox's morning "de-briefing" was, if anything, more stormy than usual – possibly because he had called it very early while it was still dark and no-one had slept enough. The fiery fox was particularly irritable – and very disturbed by the report he had received about the attack by Max the dog.

"Dogs are pretty nasty creatures," he said. "We foxes should know – they are always chasing us.

Hammy and Snuff tried to reassure him that the attack had not affected their friendship with the Human girl. Old Crow was quick to sing the praises of his squadron of sparrow hawks – and even quicker to point out that he, Old Crow, had personally trained them. He even reported how the girl Mandy had offered to let him sit on her hand.

But the brigadier was unconvinced. The Wizard's plan, he said, was looking extremely shaky. One after another, he turned on his officers, reprimanding them for the silliest of reasons. Snuff, Hammy and Old Crow were lectured in turn – each studying their toes closely while the angry fox ranted on.

Colonel Badger escaped the ordeal because he had not woken up yet – and Blink Otter escaped because he had left by boat, early in the morning, to carry on the dam-building project in the higher reaches of the stream.

Nevertheless, it was Blink Otter – or rather a messenger sent by the Admiral – who brought the briefing to an end and spared the other officers further verbal abuse from the agitated fox.

A young swift, who had been flying as fast as only a young swift can fly, burst into the room, almost too breathless to speak and causing such a commotion that even Colonel Badger awoke with a start.

"Urgent message," the swift gasped. "Urgent message from Blink Otter…"

He then had to pause to regain his breath.

Brigadier Fox was impatient. "Come on young fella," he said. "If it's urgent, we need to know now – not when you get your breath back."

The swift nodded. "Yes sir, sorry sir. I'll do my best. It's the stream – it has already been blocked…by accident."

"By accident?" demanded the irritable brigadier. "How can it be blocked by accident?"

Jumbles Wood

The swift explained. "A mattress has floated down the stream and become wedged under the fallen tree, blocking the section that Blink had left open. The water has risen overnight and is already flooding nearby fields. Soon it will be pouring down the hill – towards the Human house."

Brigadier Fox was puzzled: "What's a mattress doing in the stream?"

Colonel Badger rubbed sleep from his eyes and made one of his rare contributions.

"Some Humans are always doing it – dumping their old mattresses in rivers and streams. Dumped one near my house once, and I found it most comfortable until it got old and smelly. But it's rather stupid of the Humans really. I'm sure they have no need to do it."

"Then it will serve them right," snapped the Brigadier. "My plan was to flood the house if all else failed – this will save us the trouble."

"But, sir," cried an alarmed Hammy. "All else HASN'T failed. We are still talking to Mandy. She wants to help us and may have nearly persuaded her mother to help us too. But if the house is flooded now, we will get the blame and all our efforts will have been for nothing."

Snuff joined in: "We must warn Mandy – the Humans may be able to do something if they get a warning."

Even Old Crow agreed. "We may be able to help the Humans – in which case they might see our point of view," he cackled excitedly.

Brigadier Fox frowned. He had a long memory and was recalling the war with the animals of Green Valley, who had deceived the Jumbles Wood animals under the pretence of friendship. But his military mind was turning over rapidly and thinking of other possibilities too. He came to a quick decision.

"You are right. We must send a warning."

He turned to Old Crow. "You can get to the Human house quickest. You have talked to the girl, Mandy, so she knows you. Goodness no why, but she might even be beginning to like you. Off you go."

Old Crow's chest swelled with pride. Here, at last, was his big opportunity. The fate of the Human house, perhaps of Mandy and her family and perhaps even of the whole of Jumbles Wood, depended on him. At last, here was his chance to prove that he, Old Crow, was the most important of all the officers.

"Have no fear," he cried. "I shall go immediately. I shall not fail you. I shall…"

"Cut the cackle, you old fool!" shouted Brigadier Fox. "Get going."

Old Crow stopped his chattering, swept into the air with a flurry of his black wings was gone.

Snuff Rabbit saluted the brigadier.

"That was a good decision, sir. I think we are doing the right thing," he said.

"Hmmmmph!" responded Brigadier Fox. "We shall see. If it turns out I was wrong, and the Humans prove untrustworthy, I have more tricks up my sleeve."

CHAPTER 23

Old Crow's warning

Old Crow flew faster than he had flown for years. He arrived at the big red house to find it in darkness and apparently deserted, except for Max the dog who was asleep in his kennel. Curtains were drawn in all the windows.

For a moment, the wily bird could not think what to do. He knew he had to find Amanda, for he would not be able to give the warning to anyone else. But which room was hers?

Then he remembered something the girl had said when she was talking to Hammy and Snuff in the garden. Her window faced Jumbles Wood – and there was only one bedroom window facing in that direction.

Old Crow alighted on the window ledge and rapped sharply on the glass with his beak. There was no response so he rapped again... and again...and again. Each time he rapped harder. Finally he heard a sound from inside and the curtains were pulled back. It was Amanda.

The girl's face lit up when she saw her visitor. Gently, so as not to knock him off the window ledge, she opened the window and held out her hand.

"Old Crow, I am so pleased to see you," she said.

The Air Commodore decided there was no time to waste – and hopped on to her outstretched hand.

Amanda was delighted. "Oh, we REALLY are friends now, Old Crow. I always knew you weren't as crotchety as you sometimes seem."

"Of course I'm not," he said, in a rather crotchety tone. But then added: "I have urgent news, Mandy. There is no time to waste. The stream up the hill behind your house...it has been blocked by an old mattress and a huge flood is heading your way..."

Amanda's eyes widened. "How do you know? What will happen...?"

"Your house will be flooded unless something is done quickly – that's what will happen."

At that moment the door to Amanda's bedroom opened slightly and Robin popped his head inside.

"Who are you talking to," he began – and then stopped in amazement as he saw his sister standing by the window with the crow perched on her hand.

"Cool! You really are into this wildlife thing, aren't you! How the heck did you get that bird to come to you?"

Amanda ignored his question. All she could think about was the impending danger. "Robin – the house is going to be flooded. The stream up the back field has been blocked by an old mattress."

"What! How do you know that?"

Amanda hesitated and then blurted out: "Old Crow has just told me."

Robin put his hands on his hips and sighed. "Oh no! You're not into this talking to animals thing again, are you? Mum and Dad are worried sick you know – they think you are going crackers."

"But Robin, I'm serious. The stream has been blocked and a flood is coming this way. We've no time to waste."

Her brother sighed again.

"Right, I'll prove to you for once and for all that this is all nonsense. You must be imagining things. I can see the stream from my window – I'll go and look."

Old Crow hopped on to Amanda's shoulder and whispered in her ear: "He won't be able to see the blockage from here – but there will hardly be any water in the stream because it has burst its banks further up the hill."

Amanda blurted out: "You won't be able to see the blockage from here – but the stream will be almost empty because the water can't get through."

"We'll see," said Robin, turning and marching back into his own bedroom. He flung back the curtains and looked out.

"Crikey! You're right – the water IS low. I have never seen it so low."

"Told you so," said Amanda, who had followed him into his room with Old Crow still clinging to her shoulder.

"I'll tell Dad immediately," said Robin. "But don't say you were told by the bird or he just won't believe us…"

He ran to their parents' room while Amanda returned to her own room. "I think you'd better leave, Old Crow," she said. "Perhaps you could fly up the stream and see what's happening."

Old Crow, who had not been feeling entirely at ease inside the Human house, agreed.

"I'll let you know what's going on as soon as I can," he called, as he flew from the bedroom window.

Robin, meanwhile, had aroused his parents. He managed to avoid answering when his father asked: "How did you find out?" He just pointed to the almost dry stream bed.

Harry Watson reacted quickly.

"There's certainly something strange going on. I'll get the Land Rover and drive up the field," he said. "If I follow the stream I should be able to find the blockage and if it's only an old mattress I should be able to shift it. You'd better come too, Robin."

As Father was starting the engine, Amanda came running from the house. "Can I come too?" she shouted.

"Jump in – you might be able to help."

Father swung the Land Rover out into the lane and waited, impatiently as Robin opened the five barred gate leading to the field opposite the house. Then he drove up the steeply sloping field, keeping as close as possible to the stream.

The sturdy vehicle bumped its way over the rough ground onwards and upwards, its headlights piercing the gloom. Amanda, sitting in the back, had to hold on tight to prevent herself being thrown around. Robin and her father were keeping their eyes on the stream, looking for any sign of a blockage. But she had her eyes on the sky.

Suddenly she saw a black shape swooping low to the right of the Land Rover. It was Old Crow. As he swept passed she heard his cackling voice cry: "Hurry – there's not much time!"

"What on earth was that noise?" Father said, struggling with the steering wheel as the vehicle hit a particularly bumpy stretch of field.

"I think it was a bird," said Robin. He stared at Amanda – but she said nothing.

Just ahead, a fallen tree loomed into view, a tangle of broken branches lying across the stream. "This looks like it," said Father, revving the engine. Then, as the Land Rover lurched up a steep bank, he swore – which was very unusual for Father – as the full extent of the danger came into view.

A large mattress was wedged under the tree, partially hidden by a mass of branches and other debris which had been washed down the stream. The fast flowing water, coming from further up the hill, had been diverted out of its normal course and had formed another stream which was emptying into a large, saucer-shaped meadow which, in turn, had been transformed into a lake.

The water level had almost reached the rim of the "saucer" – and when it did he could see it would pour down the hillside towards the house.

Jumbles Wood

"There must be hundreds of thousands of gallons there," gasped Father. "It's enough to sweep the house away. We've got to clear that blockage – and we've got to do it fast."

Jumbles Wood

CHAPTER 24

Robin to the rescue

Harry Watson brought the Land Rover to a sliding halt as close as he could get to the fallen tree and jumped out, followed by Robin and Amanda.

Upstream of the blockage the stream, normally fairly shallow at this point, had become a deep cauldron of surging water, swirling around until it found its new route and then pouring into the saucer-shaped meadow.

Father sized up the situation swiftly. "We've really got to shift the tree," he shouted, above the sound of the water. "If we just move the mattress it will just block up again. In fact, it looks as if it would have blocked up soon even without the mattress."

He brought a length of thick rope from the back of the Land Rover.

"We'll need to attach this to the far end of the tree – this end is firmly wedged."

Robin said: "I could climb across and tie the rope on."

Father hesitated – then realised that his son probably would be able to climb through the maze of branches faster than he could.

"OK – but be careful. We don't want you falling in."

He tied the rope loosely around Robin's waist to leave both the boy's hands free for the climb.

Amanda watched nervously as her brother began to clamber along the trunk of the fallen tree, sometimes crawling to get between branches. Twice he lost his footing and nearly fell, but on both occasions he was able to grab a sturdy branch and steady himself before carrying on. Father paid out the rope, making sure it did not become entangled in the branches.

Eventually Robin reached the other side, untied the rope from his waist and tied it securely to the main trunk of the fallen tree. Then he clambered back across the stream, moving more quickly and with increasing confidence.

Safely back on the bank, he shouted: "Right, Dad. Let's get it moved."

Father had already attached the rope to the Land Rover. Now he revved the engine and put the vehicle into gear. As the rope tightened, the wheels skidded for a moment on the muddy turf but then gripped. The tree began to move – and water began to trickle back into the dry stream bed. Father accelerated more and, suddenly, the tree was high and dry on the bank. The water cascaded back into its original course – and gradually the new stream flooding the meadow reduced to a trickle and then stopped.

"Phew!" exclaimed Father. "We've done it!"

A black shape wheeled overhead and Amanda heard a familiar voice screech: "You've done it!"

Father glanced up. "Odd, the way that bird is behaving," he said.

Then he waded into the now much calmer stream and pulled the old mattress onto the bank.

"I wish the people who dump things in streams would realise the trouble they can cause," he said. "We could have lost our home just because some lazy so-and-so couldn't be bothered taking an old mattress to a proper tip site."

Amanda looked at the new lake which filled the meadow. "What will happen to all that water, Dad?" she asked.

"It will soak away, eventually. Probably take a couple of weeks to dry out completely, but it's no danger to us now."

As they drove back, slowly, down the hill towards the house, Father said: "Robin, you never did tell me how you found out about the blockage in the stream."

The boy hesitated – but Amanda spoke up: "I told him," she said.

"Oh – and who told you? One of your animal friends, I suppose."

"That's right – that bird that kept circling above us all the time. The one you said was behaving oddly."

Father thought for a moment. Then he said, quietly: "Well, we certainly owe him something, Mandy. This is a good time to tell you I've decided not to build any more houses here. We'll just finish off the one we have started, so that we will have a neighbour.

"But a lady from the village has asked me to let her graze ponies on the rest of the land, leading down to the wood. She is prepared to pay a good rate, so we'll have a useful income from the field."

Amanda was overjoyed. "Does that mean that Jumbles Wood will be saved – and that we'll have ponies living next to us?"

"That's right. I've decided it wouldn't be a good idea to build more houses here anyway. The stream is more prone to flooding than I had realised so there would always be a risk to the new houses."

"Stop the car," said Amanda. "I want to get out a moment."

A new day was dawning as she stood next to the Land Rover, looking upwards to where a lone black shape was wheeling and diving against a lightening sky.

"Old Crow," she shouted. "No more houses will be built and Jumbles Wood is safe."

The lively jackdaw swooped low over the vehicle. Father and Robin heard it screech before it turned, climbed in the sky and headed off in the direction of Jumbles Wood.

But Amanda clearly heard the words: "Thank you, Mandy – I'll spread the news."

"Remarkable," said Father, watching the disappearing bird. "Quite remarkable."

CHAPTER 25

And finally

In the days that followed, changes began to occur in and around the big red house. Father decided it would be better if Max lived inside the house with the family, rather than in a kennel. Max seemed to like the idea because he immediately started to become a much more friendly dog.

Robin decided he was too old to play with toy soldiers any more. He dismantled his fort and threw all his soldiers, tanks and guns into a box which he put at the back of the garden shed, just in case he changed his mind later.

Father's workmen broke off from working on the house next door and erected a fence around the field leading down to Jumbles Wood. The first ponies arrived and Amanda thought they were beautiful. The lady who owned them promised that she could ride them whenever she wanted – once she had learned to ride properly.

In the meadow above the house, the flood water gradually subsided and Father said it would soon have gone altogether.

But one thing happened that made Amanda unhappy. The daily visits from Hammy, Snuff and Old Crow stopped. There was no sign of them.

Then, one morning, she looked out of the window and saw the guinea pig's friendly little face peeping around a bush. She was overjoyed – and ran out into the garden immediately.

"Oh, Hammy! It's wonderful to see you again. I thought you had forgotten about me."

"Sorry," said the guinea pig. "I wanted to come earlier, but we have been pretty busy in Jumbles Wood. Brigadier Fox has kept us all on the go, patrolling, training, drilling and generally playing at soldiers. That's what he's like, you know."

"But doesn't he know Jumbles Wood is safe now – didn't Old Crow deliver the message?"

"Oh yes, he's been told. But he has a military mind. He wouldn't believe it at first. Said it could all be a trick. It was only when the fences went up and the ponies appeared that he was prepared to accept that the houses were not going to be built.

"Now he is going on about demobilisation, whatever that means. He says we all have to prepare for a return to civilian life. But that's Brigadier Fox – he's like that."

Hammy paused. "But the real reason I have come to see you is that today is the last day we will be able to talk to each other – the Wizard's spell is due to wear off."

Amanda smiled. "I'm sure we'll always be able to understand each other now, Hammy. We won't need the Wizard's spell."

"I'm sure too – but we won't be able to talk. I thought there might be things we would like to say before the spell is broken."

"There are lots of things," said Amanda. "I would never have enough time to say everything, but most important thing I want to tell you is that I understand that you would never want to come back and live in a hutch. I just hope you will carry on coming to see me – and I want to be able to come and see you, and Snuff and Old Crow and all the other animals and birds I have never even met.

"Will you take me to see Snuff's Oak, and Crow's Nest Hill and all the other places I have heard about? Then I will be able to come and see you anytime I want."

"Of course I will – and of course we will all carry on coming to see you here."

Amanda told Mother she was going for a walk and soon, guided by Hammy, she was plunging into the heart of Jumbles Wood. She saw Old Crow's house at Crow's Next Hill and the little dairy on the banks of Deep River where Blink Otter worked as a milkman.

And finally she arrived at the clearing by Snuff's Oak where all the animals and birds of the Jumbles Wood Army were waiting to greet her.

Brigadier Fox stood proudly to attention and saluted. Blink Otter became so excited that he blinked faster and more furiously than ever before.

He said: "I am the only one given the power to speak to you who never got the chance..." and broke down in tears.

Amanda stroked his sleek, shiny fur and told him: "You are the most beautiful otter I have ever seen."

Old Crow flapped his wings importantly and started to explain just how important he was...until Old Badger, more wide-awake than he had been in years, managed to tell him to be quiet.

Snuff Rabbit waited until every other animal had been introduced to Amanda. Then he shyly stepped forward and held out a paw.

"I would love to show you inside my house, Mandy," he said. "But I am afraid you are too big to fit in."

Amanda laughed. "I know, Snuff. I would love to be able to go inside too. But unless we can get the Wizard to cast another spell – to make me small – I never can.

"But I can imagine what it is like. Hammy has told me a lot about it. Your cosy little parlour, your Grandfather clock and your clean and tidy kitchen. I can imagine what it is all like. Even the Brigadier's office with the big desk."

Snuff blushed as the girl stroke his head gently.

"Snuff's Oak will be Hammy's home too from now on," he said. "We will always be pleased to see you – and we will come to visit you too. We will be friends forever."

Amanda walked home alone. She felt happy, sad and proud all at the same time.

Tomorrow, she knew, she would no longer be able to talk to the animals of Jumbles Wood – but she would still understand them better than anyone else in the world.

THE END

Old Crow's Dictionary

Many words have more than one meaning, but Old Crow's Dictionary gives the meaning used in this book. If you want to know more about the meaning of these, or any other words, there are plenty of dictionaries around that are better than Old Crow's. But don't tell him!

Abruptly. Suddenly and unexpectedly, perhaps unpleasantly

Absurd. Ridiculous, silly or stupid

Acquaintance. A person you know, but not very well.

Admiral. Chief commander of a navy

Aerial. Something happening In the air.

Airborne. Something travelling by air

Arrogant. Overbearing and bossy in a nasty way

Bedraggled. Untidy and dirty.

Beret. A flat, round cap worn by soldiers and others

Brigade. A group of soldiers within an army

Brigadier. An army officer of quite high rank

Brusquely. Abrupt in manner

Cauldron. An area of bubbling, swirling water

Jumbles Wood

Corporal. A lower rank in the army, just above that of private

De-briefing. Gathering information from soldiers

Demobilisation. Disbanding an army after a war

Deploy. To place soldiers in position

Disdain. A feeling of scorn

Elaborate. Highly detailed, complicated.

Enlist. To join the army

Expedition. A journey into the unknown

Fugitive. Someone who is being hunted

Glower. An angry or fierce stare

Hare-brained. A silly idea not likely to work

Humiliated. Feeling ashamed and humble.

Imminent. Something that is going to happen soon

Ingredients. Parts of a mixture of things

Instinctively. Something you do naturally without thinking

Intelligence. Information about the enemy.

Invariably. Something that never alters.

Khaki. Brownish colour used for army uniforms

Liaison. Being in touch with other people.

Major. An officer in the army.

Military. To do with soldiers, armies or war.

Mobilise. To get an army ready for war.

Obstinately. Stubborn, very firm, not prepared to change

Partial. Being rather fond of something.

Platoon. Small group of soldiers within an army

Pomposity. Putting on show of dignity.

Ponderously. Moving slowly and heavily.

Prefaced. Something which comes first

Jumbles Wood

Privileges. A happy advantage over other people

Prone. Inclined or likely to happen

Prostrate. Lying flat on your back on the ground.

Psychiatrist. A doctor who treats mental illness

Quarry. A hunted animal.

Rank. A position in an army, navy or air force

Reclining. Lying comfortably on your back

Reconnaissance. Checking up on the enemy.

Relented. To give way to someone else's opinion

Reprimand. To discipline or tell someone off

Resplendent. Dressed to look splendid

Retorted. To answer someone sharply or indignantly

Sett. A burrow, or hole, where a badger lives

Shirk. To avoid or get out of doing something

Squadron. A group of aircraft within an air force

Strategy. An overall plan.

Sympathetic. Understanding or feeling sorry for someone.

Synchronise. To set clocks or watches so they all show the same time

Uncivil. Not being kind or polite to people

Ushered. To show someone in or out of somewhere

Wily. Being very wise or cunning

Wince. Pulling a face to show pain or embarrassment.

Don't Forget...

You can learn more about Jumbles Wood and its inhabitants and find out what is going on there now, simply by visiting:

www.jumbleswood.com

Printed in the United Kingdom
by Lightning Source UK Ltd.
126240UK00001B/214-507/A